WHAT PRICE B

"The Green Age works toward the grea____ ___ Moon touched Jill's arm gently. "Believe me, the midwest will bloom again, but it will take many years. More pressing matters concern us today—like feeding the world's hungry. Pacifica is part of the answer. Beaumont plans to use Pacifica to seize economic control of the world. The Pacifica technology must be shared, not kept secret for the benefit of one greedy man."

Pacifica—that word was a magic phrase around Beaumont Industries, Jill knew. The boss's pet project, very hush-hush even in the corporate offices, was rumored to be A.J.'s newest license to print money.

Jill stubbornly shook her head. She didn't want to get sucked into this mess. It wasn't fair. All she'd ever wanted was a safe, quiet life for herself and her family. But how could they have that life anymore with famine, energy shortages, rioting, and the likelihood that her parents could soon lose their farm?

"I don't even know what Pacifica *is*," she said. "How could I help you?"

Jade Moon didn't seem to hear. She opened her emerald-sequined purse and pulled out an envelope. "One hundred thousand dollars, plus we'll give you a regular monthly salary . . . enough to pay all your parents' bills, enough to help your other relatives. Take it, Jill, you need it. All you have to do is keep your eyes open for us. Anything you can find out about Pacifica will be of interest."

So much money . . .

If Pacifica would make Beaumont even richer while the rest of the world suffered, why shouldn't she help Jade and the Green Agers? Why should her family live in poverty and despair? Wouldn't it be best if the world shared Pacifica's technology—whatever it was? She felt torn and ashamed for being tempted.

Jade Moon thrust the envelope into her hands, and Jill took it automatically. She thought of Judas, the betrayer, but Beaumont was more like Pontius Pilate than Christ.

Smiling sweetly, Jade Moon said, "You *are* going to be helping the whole world."

PACIFICA

JOHN GREGORY BETANCOURT

& LINDA E. BUSHYAGER

WILDSIDE PRESS

PACIFICA

An original publication of Wildside Press. For more information, contact:

Wildside Press
P.O. Box 301
Holicong, PA 18928-0301

First Edition: July 2002

ONE

SHE SWIRLED up to Cristopher Morrisey in a knot of friends and hangers-on, her skin painted chocolate and azure, her hair a shimmering golden bow. A blue-green holodress twined snakelike around her, revealing dark thighs and the occasional smooth curve of breast, but Marica Vonn-Grendel was like that, and Cris expected it of her. It was part of her charm, part of her power, all of which drew him inexorably closer, a moth to her flame. After all, what did he, a mere painter, mere *artist*, know of fashion? Only her eyes seemed normal tonight, that pale piercing shade of blue he'd always found so distracting.

"Cristopher *darling*," she said, and when she smiled her teeth were dark as her skin, crawling with geometric designs.

"Marica," he said. "I didn't expect you. I thought my gallery openings were too tame for your tastes."

"Wifely duties," she said, and a titter came from her coterie of friends. Cris glared and they shut up. They too sported weird holographic clothes and wild, dyed chromatic hair designs. He remembered none of their names. Just glitterfolk, like Marica; they came and went and others would replace them in an endless, mindless flow.

He forced a smile. "Of course, your portrait. I'd forgotten it's on exhibit." She hadn't been his wife in months, he reminded himself, not since he'd finished painting her. That portrait hung on the far wall, a masterful study in oil and holo laserwork, five meters high and ten wide: Marica, naked on a beach, with gulls constantly wheeling overhead, the interplay of shadows on her face the piece's focal point. It was his greatest work thus far. Something about Marica inspired him as no other woman ever had. Or, he thought, ever would again.

A lull in talk around them brought the gulls' raucous voices. After Marica abandoned him, he'd dubbed crow caws into the audio track. It made an interesting contrast to his usual hyper-realism.

"I'm having a party later tonight. Come?"

"I don't know . . ."

Her lips pursed, a mock kiss. "I'll send someone to pick you up, dear. Ta." And off she swept, followed by her glitterdressed friends, to make a quick circuit of the room. He doubted she'd even remember having asked him to her party in an hour; but that was the way she'd always been. He'd known that when he'd proposed in January. Still, their four months together while he'd dawdled over her portrait had been more than most of her lovers enjoyed.

As they passed Cris on their way to the exit, something small and white dropped from Marica's hand.

They'd gone by the time he crossed the floor and picked up the paper. Someone (surely not Marica) had neatly inked PACIFICA in all caps.

He crumpled it up. Then something made him smooth it out, read that single word again. With a sigh he put the card in his breast pocket, next to his heart, and tried to force her from his thoughts for the rest of the evening.

Accepting a glass of wine from one of the wandering servants, he put on his charm and began to mingle with patrons. Mega-money everywhere; no telling where his next sale or commission would come from.

A pair of green-haired old ladies with too much makeup cornered him by his holostatue of starships crashing into the sun. "You're a genius," the one on the left cooed, "the last artist who actually *feels* the human condition."

"Thank you," he murmured as she nattered on and on, "you're too kind." His gaze kept straying back to the door, to where he'd last seen Marica, and he felt a strange, empty sort of longing inside.

Idly he fingered his pocket. He pictured Marica's tall form moving away from him in a swirl of color, her dress the blue-green on the sea, her hair the blond-gold of the morning sun, the strange card fluttering down from her hand like the falling petal of a flower.

Pacifica. He wondered what it meant.

*   *   *

When his opening ended two hours later, he wandered slightly drunk, slightly melancholy out onto the gallery's roof-top parking lot for a breath of fresh air. To his surprise, the glitterfolk had waited for him. They had some sort of large new helijet taking up half a dozen parking spaces, and the noise of the party inside the heejee grated like the squawking of strident crows. Its exterior rippled under holographic projections, looking first like an eighteenth century sailing ship, then a colorful South American banana boat, then back again in a looped cycle.

The door swung open and Jade Moon, one of the few of Marica's friends he remembered (more for her green-dyed face than anything else), took his arm and pulled him inside.

"I feel alienated," she announced proudly. "That's what we're doing tonight."

"Good for you," Cris said.

He pushed deeper into the heejee's main compartment. Holograms had transformed it into a small, chandeliered ballroom. Holoed geometric designs flickered everywhere, blinding, revealing, blinding. Everyone wore paper masks of dead performers' faces. He wandered through the Marilyns, the Elvises, the Madonnas. He didn't see Marica anywhere, so he moved into the next room. Here dancers swayed, beckoning, undulating to the pulsing beat of glaze-rock. Drugmists hazed the air; his head swam dizzily.

Jade Moon came up to him again and tried to get him to join the dance. Slender and attractive, she had always struck Cris as more intelligent than most of the glitterfolk. But Marica was the only woman on his mind. He disengaged Jade Moon's arms and continued his search.

Finally, static crackling around him, he pushed through the soundguard into the quiet cockpit. All alone, Marica stood looking out across the city's lights. She turned when he cleared his throat, and he saw she'd been crying.

"What's wrong?" he asked.

"We're so alone in the world." She stepped close and leaned her head against his shoulder.

Alienation tonight. He hesitated a second, then pulled her tight, hugging her like she'd never left, never terminated their marriage, never abandoned him. God, it felt good. For a second the months were reeling back, and she was *his* again and they were in love, the two of them against the world.

Then, remembering the pain of loss as she grew bored and drifted away, he bit his lip and forced himself back.

"No, Marica," he said. "Not again. Not this time."

She sagged, and he let her collapse at his feet. Softly she began to sob.

Cris didn't know what to do. *Alienation.* It was another fad among the glitterfolk, ultimately meaningless. And, he reminded himself, sure to pass by tomorrow night. *But for now she needs me. For now . . .*

He couldn't help himself. He knelt and hugged her, and once more experienced that strange sense of fulfillment he only found at her side.

"Could you fly us home?" she asked.

"This thing? Are you crazy? I'd never get it off the ground!"

"You used to fly them in the Air Force. And the man who sold it to me said it would handle exactly like a regular heejee—it only looks so big because of the holos."

"I haven't flown in years; besides, what happened to—what's his name? Your pilot. Kyan, isn't it?"

"Drunk." She shrugged. "We locked him in the closet till he sobers up. Nobody else can pilot, so I waited for you." She gestured vaguely north, toward her estate. "You'll fly us home, won't you? Please?"

He bent to kiss her, but she pushed him away, laughing now. "Just friends."

"I need to paint you."

"You already did."

"I need to do it again. For me, not the gallery this time. So I can remember you."

"Just friends," she repeated.

Each word felt like another nail being driven into his coffin. Angrily he thought, It's like we never had anything between us. But still he dared hope that she would somehow grow up, that he could somehow change enough to be accepted again.

So he sighed and slid into the pilot's seat. The safety harness buckled across his chest, and when he took the controls, digital readouts flickered to life around him. It seemed simple enough, like a heejee but with extra jets to compensate for the added mass of the party rooms. He didn't think he'd have much trouble, especially with computer control.

The engines powered up smoothly. A low, gravelly hum spread through the cockpit like a familiar melody he had not heard for years, and it sounded good. Lights began to blink green across the instrument panel. When he put his hands on the controls he felt a surge of exhilaration. Flying was like bicycling, you never forgot how. He hadn't thought he missed it, but sitting in the cockpit again, he realized he had.

A snatch of bellowed lyrics came through the soundguard— *And let the people blaze // Burning off another scar*—He wondered at that, whether the words held any special meaning for him. He needed his scars.

"Alienation," Marica whispered to herself, over and over like some secret mantra: "Alienation—alienation—alienation . . ."

Cris sighed. As he lifted from the gallery's roof, he logged into City Control and punched in their destination.

"Roger, PCX-440," a man's voice said, "we have you. Flight path approved. Switching to computer control now."

Slowly the huge helijet steered north, toward Marica's home. Cris sat back, gazing into the darkness with an artist's eye, studying the hypnotic blur of lights passing below.

This is a mistake, he thought once, in a moment of rare, rational introspection. *She's going to hurt me again.* Only he couldn't make himself care. *As long as I'm with her . . .*

Throughout the flight, Marica wandered in and out of the cockpit, sometimes laughing, sometimes crying, her mood swinging rapidly through the phases of her alienation.

Once Cris asked her, "Are you happy?"

She laughed and countered, "Are *you?*"

I could be, Cris wanted to say, but he didn't. That might upset her, and upsetting her might screw up their chances of getting together again. At least she'd brought him home with her, and perhaps that meant something. She hadn't taken a new lover yet, as far as he could tell, so he could still hope, still dream of her.

He felt the card she'd dropped through the fabric of his shirt. He wondered if he should return it. *Pacifica.* What did it mean?

As they left City Control's airspace, he had to take manual control and pay more attention. The large heejee lumbered like a bloated airborne elephant.

He leaned back and concentrated on keeping on course. Blocks of suburban housing flowed away below, dark for the most part because of power rationing.

*   *   *

Half an hour later, they crossed the high stone fence bordering Marica's estate. Cris locked into the house computer and opened a window through the estate's defenses. Slowly he circled down toward the sprawling mansion that served as the main house. Floodlights bathed the beautifully manicured grounds in pastel pinks and blues. Only a few small heejees sat on the rooftop heliport.

Marica wandered back into the cockpit and sat beside him.

"Land on the ground," she said. "There won't be enough space for my guests if you park on the roof."

He picked one of the tennis courts and toggled the automatic landing sequence. Marica watched as Cris unstrapped himself, then took his arm and escorted him through the heejee to the main doors.

"Alienation," she told him slowly, with great affected sighs, "can make you happy."

Abruptly, she screamed joyously, launching herself into the crowd.

Cris jumped, caught by surprise, and when the glitterfolk began to applaud and gather around, he cursed them. But it was Marica who drew his eye, and he couldn't push her from his thoughts no matter how he tried.

TWO

JILL WASHINGTON checked the helijet's controls for what seemed the thousandth time in the last five minutes. The engines hummed powerfully, and the onboard diagnostics checked green-for-go, so she knew she could lift at any moment. But still she hesitated. Something didn't feel right. *Damn if I'm ever going to get used to this one,* she thought.

The heejee itself didn't bother her; Jill had flown helijets hundreds of times in her three years as a pilot, and before that she'd spent four years in the Air Force, distributing food for the United Nations. Rather, it was the smiling thirty-year-old belted into the passenger's seat next to her, one Alexander James Beaumont, who made her nervous, not to mention Beaumont's two stone-faced bodyguards in the back.

Jill risked a sideways glance. A.J. Beaumont had that blond-haired, blue-eyed, all-American look of which movie stars dream, right down to a cowlick across his forehead and perfect ivory teeth. His round, boyish face made him look at least five years younger than his age. Tonight he wore a white double-breasted silk suit, doubtless hand-tailored to the last stitch, and doubtless costing more than Jill made in a month.

Indeed, Jill thought sourly, Beaumont looked model-perfect, just a rich playboy out for an evening's sport in all the posh nightclubs. But she knew Beaumont had something else in mind.

According to rumor, Alexander James Beaumont never did anything for pleasure, at least pleasure as Jill understood it. Rather, his passions ran toward power and money—power to control other people, and money to get that power.

That sweetly cherubic young face hid a savage mind. You didn't offend Beaumont; his temper-tantrums were legendary. Rumor said Beaumont had once beaten a chauffeur to death with a tire iron for a fender-scrape in a parking lot.

And that's what I am, Jill thought, *a glorified chauffeur for the great A.J. Beaumont.*

And where most people would have ridden in the passenger compartment, leaving the pilot to do her work, Beaumont had chosen to sit up front, next to her. He watched her every move with the intensity of a lion on the prowl. It made her nervous, but of course she couldn't complain. She didn't dare. With the midwestern drought going on five years now, and Missouri looking more like a desert than the breadbasket it was supposed to be, her parents weren't doing so well. They needed the money she sent every month. If she got fired . . . well, the unemployment lines were already full from the New Depression, and a midwestern drought only made things worse. You could barely find honest work these days; people clung to any job they had.

Jill couldn't risk it. She *would* stay, and she *would* enjoy it. Or else.

"Anything wrong?" Beaumont asked suddenly. His voice sounded high, almost childlike and innocent against the whine of the engines. "I'm in a hurry, you know."

Jill shook her head. "Nothing wrong, sir. I want to get you there safe and sound. Everything checks now."

But something did bother her. As if recently getting assigned to Beaumont as his personal chauffeur weren't bad enough, a couple of Green Age activists had tried to bribe her the previous night. As if she could ever access Beaumont's secrets!

She didn't want to think about it. She had a job to do. Pushing everything else from her mind, she toggled the microphone at her throat.

"I have a go, Control," she said.

"Roger, heejee GBI-1," a woman's voice said in her right ear. "You're cleared."

Jill upped power and gentled the helijet from the deck of the *Lady Pecunia*, Beaumont's huge luxury yacht. After an easy turn eastward, they accelerated to cruising speed. Moon and stars overhead cast a pleasant glow across the waves, and here and there patches of algae gleamed with a pale phosphorescence.

Despite the ocean's beauty, she looked forward to reaching dry land. No Washington had gone to sea willingly since the first of the line had been trapped by Gold Coast slavers some two-hundred-odd years before. Of course things had changed since the bad old days; but the family dread of sea and ships remained, like some faint, half-remembered nightmare.

With all her safety checks run, Jill didn't have much to do for the next hour. Slowly her thoughts crept back to the night before. She'd been offered a lot of money to spy on A.J. Beaumont. Enough that her parents wouldn't ever have to worry about food or water or anything else ever again. Enough that it had tempted her more than it should have.

She risked another glance at her boss. Beaumont had hunched around to face the window. He'd made it clear on the flight out to the *Pecunia* that morning that he didn't enjoy idle talk, so after they'd taken off they'd traveled in silence, him lost in thought and gazing into space, Jill listening to the roar of jets and the whisper of wind and the slow, steady ticking of instruments, with the two bodyguards silent as mummies in the back.

Of course she'd turned down the Green Age offer to spy on Beaumont. It had seemed more amusing than anything else at the time. But now thoughts of what all that money could have done for her family kept coming back to haunt her. *How much do I really owe Beaumont, anyway?* she wondered.

Still, despite all the stories and rumors, and a little eccentric behavior like refusing to talk to her while they flew, A.J. Beaumont hadn't seemed all that bad. He'd actually been quite charming the first time they'd met; he had a certain raw magnetism, a certain charisma, and she could see why people stayed with him.

No, she finally decided, she'd done the right thing. She might not like everything about A.J. Beaumont, but he was her employer. Her parents were solid Missouri Baptists, and they'd passed their strict code of ethics on to her.

If only it hadn't been *so much* money . . .

Why hadn't she told Beaumont about the bribery attempt? Jill found she didn't quite know. Beaumont might have rewarded her for loyalty. She should have told him immediately. She should be telling him now. Yet something made her hesitate.

Keep your head down. Don't make trouble. She'd lived her whole life by those two simple rules. If you did your job, you'd make it through all right in the end.

Or, she wondered, was she still considering the offer in the back of her mind? The idea worried her. *So much money.*

Beaumont seemed to be staring intently at the ocean. Since there was nothing to see yet, except open water for the next half hour until they got to New York, Jill wondered what fascinated her boss. She didn't understand him and thought she probably never would.

Perhaps he'll get tired of me. He can ask for another personal pilot any time he wants. That might be best, if she could keep her job at Beaumont Industries.

For now, she'd stick it out. Perhaps a bit of Beaumont's fortune would rub off on her if she worked hard. A.J. Beaumont had a well-documented knack for taking what he wanted in wildly pyrotechnic ways. And he wanted a lot. In the ten years since he inherited a small financial empire from his parents, Beaumont had parlayed his stake from a few hundred million to over forty *billion* dollars.

It seemed an obscene amount of money. Jill couldn't conceive of that much except in the most general way, as a string of zeroes on a piece of paper. No human had any business with that much. Beaumont would never be able to spend it all, no matter what he did.

Beaumont Industries owned casinos, orbiting satellites, banks, pollution-control companies, petroleum refineries, movie studios, and much more. You name it, they owned it. Hell, Jill thought, sometimes it seemed Beaumont Industries owned half the planet. And for all that, A.J. Beaumont still paid his employees as poorly as every other tightfisted tycoon ever born. Jill would have welcomed a few thousand more each payday.

I could have had it, she thought. The Green Agers didn't want that much: just for her to keep her eyes open, rummage in the trash, perhaps copy a few documents if the chance arose. It wasn't even industrial espionage, they had said. It was all for a good cause . . . .

Abruptly Jill's attention snapped back to the heejee. New York's skyline had appeared as if by magic; she'd been flying more by reflex than anything else. No harm done this time; Beaumont still ruminated in silence.

New York City glowed with light, and heejees zipped like a thousand fireflies overhead. Looking at it from this distance, you never would have guessed Manhattan rationed its power. Thirty million people kept it bright all night long.

Abruptly A.J. turned and asked, "Is everything taken care of? How long till we get there?"

"Yes, sir," Jill said, fingers dancing across the controls. Digital readouts changed. "The flight was punched into the New York tracking system when we left your yacht. Computer estimates endpoint arrival at eight-thirty."

"Eight-thirty exactly?"

"Eight thirty-four, exactly."

"Always be precise. I hate sloppy numbers. I don't want to have to tell you again." He sounded almost petulant.

"Yes, sir. Precise." *That's why you're the billionaire, and I'm hacking heejees. You arrogant bastard.*

A.J. Beaumont turned and once more gazed unseeingly out his window. Jill could almost see the cogs turning inside his head, plots within financial plots.

It would serve him right for someone to take him down a peg or two.

The helijet banked to the left, heading north toward the sprawling Long Island estates where the mega-rich like Alexander James Beaumont lived. Jill knew that Beaumont didn't have a mansion; he lived exclusively on his fleet of luxury yachts these days. It took someone rich and *important* to get A.J. onto land this late at night. Jill wondered who it was.

What's going on in that little mind?

*   *   *

Ten minutes later, the computer chimed. A.J. stretched and sat up straighter, knowing they'd reached the Vonn-Grendel estate.

A.J. had been seeing Marica Vonn-Grendel for the last couple months, wrangling invites to her parties, arranging chance encounters on the street, bribing mutual acquaintances to mention his name at appropriate moments. Finally he and Marica had gotten together for dinner a few weeks ago, which had led to a torrid fling aboard his yacht, which had led to tonight's party . . . and tonight's anticipated announcement.

As his chauffeur carefully listened to her headphones, she turned to him and said, "Their computer is warning us away. I can see artillery on the roof. Should I back off?"

Over the last few years every Long Island estate had become an armed camp as the rich dug themselves in. A.J. had seen it coming and gone to live at sea instead. Happily he'd been right; these days nobody on land was safe, not even in posh suburbs like these. Everyone you saw on the streets would be carrying weapons of some sort, and violence was the rule rather than the exception. That's why he had Hollis and Giacco with him, two of his bodyguards. Bodyguards had saved his life at least twice in Manhattan, and once in Los Angeles.

The weapons on the roof didn't bother A.J. He said, "Keep circling, Washington. I'll take care of everything."

Of course Marica had given him access to her estate. A.J. swung around one of his helijet's computer keypads, opened a link to the estate's computer, and punched in the entrance code. The estate's defenses acknowledged at once.

A.J. sat back and smiled smugly. He found everything with Marica so very predictable, right down to her most closely guarded secret, the code to her defenses: *ME ME ME.*

His heejee flew right in. It circled once, then set down atop the main building.

Curiously, A.J. noticed only a few small heejees occupying the rooftop landing-pads. The company logos marked them as catering vehicles. He felt a moment's apprehension, but pushed it aside. Perhaps she'd changed the party to a more *intimate* affair, for the two of them. She'd *better* be waiting inside, he thought.

"Stay here," he told his pilot as he climbed out. His two bodyguards followed, trailing at a respectful distance.

Spillage from skylights cast the roof in a sort of perpetual dusk. Although he'd been here before, it took a moment to get his bearings. The elevators stood to the left. But tonight holographic projectors had turned them into giant gargoyles. One grotesque face split down the middle as he watched, revealing an elevator car. He strode over and entered without a second's hesitation, bodyguards following like shadows.

The elevator started down at once. There were no buttons, nothing to bother the easily confused glitterfolk. Leather padded the walls, floor, and ceiling. You couldn't hurt yourself here no matter how hard you tried; you merely got on, and it carried you down.

Beaumont smiled unpleasantly. Yes, it suited dim-witted Marica and her dim-witted friends. How she ever managed to accumulate ten billion dollars in shipping company assets . . .

Be polite, he reminded himself. *You need her. She's the key to doubling your fortune overnight.*

The elevator opened onto a banquet hall set up for tonight's party. Hundreds of champagne bottles sat chilling in huge tureens of ice. Fancy bird-shaped pastries, larger than life, posed beneath sheets of plastic, or lay with multi-colored wings outspread on huge gold trays. Flaming braziers stood ready to warm hot hors d'oeuvres rushed from the kitchen ovens. In these days of food rationing, it was an opulent display of wealth and power. The champagne was a special treat; since the climatic changes had ravaged France's vineyards, about the best you could get was Norwegian sparkling wine . . . a pale alternative.

Several attendants in black tuxedos snapped to attention as he approached. Each man's hair had been dyed in rainbow-colored streaks. The head butler, resplendent in black tails, white gloves, and white bow tie, rushed to A.J.'s side.

"Where is she?" A.J. demanded.

The butler spread his hands apologetically. "Off with her friends, I'm afraid, Mr. Beaumont. She comes and goes at whim without informing the staff, so there is nothing to do but wait. She might take hours to get here, or she might nor arrive at all. We have no way of knowing, sir. May I get you a drink?"

"A sherry, and make it quick."

"Very good, sir."

And A.J. Beaumont, who had never waited for anything or anyone in his life, began to fume.

*   *   *

Jill Washington busied herself with her helijet, first wiping off the windshield and side viewports, then rubbing down the chrome grillwork. It took fifteen minutes to make everything military spit-and-polish shiny, and then she found herself with nothing to do. The onboard computer took care of the engine; she had nothing to check, and nothing further to clean. Being alone drove her crazy. She realized she needed company.

Jill looked across the dimly lighted roof, toward the various artillery stations. Behind the dark snouts of guns she could see hulking human shapes.

"Hey guys," she called. "How's it going?"

They didn't reply. Brushing back a strand of long black hair that had gotten lose from her braid, she walked toward them. When she drew close, she found the shapes weren't human at all, but mannequins propped menacingly behind the computer-controlled guns. She squinted. Someone with a sick sense of humor had painted huge, goofy grins across their faces.

She chuckled. It reminded her of the sort of gallows humor she'd seen during her days in the Air Force.

Those had been good times in their own way. All decisions made for you—what to do, where to live, what to eat—no confusing worries about right or wrong. Everything had seemed so much simpler back then.

A deep, throaty roar overhead drew her from her memories. Rooftop spotlights blazed, revealing several large circling heejees. The largest flickering with holograms that made it look like a Greek temple. They began to land, some on the rooftop pads, some on the ground below.

The party was about to begin.

THREE

INSIDE MARICA'S heejee, the music had started again, now weirdly atonal, full of drums and primitive rhythms. Holographic projections flickered over gyrating dancers. Cris glanced at Marica and found her sheathed in a Betty Boop hologram, dancing with her eyes closed, as though she were the only one in the room.

That got him moving. He located the environmental controls and tabbed off all the holos. Without them the room became an ordinary heejee compartment, fairly small and dingy. Glitterfolk called protests, but Cris ignored them.

As windows faded from oceanfront to tinted glass, he found himself gazing out onto a fairy-tale pink and blue landscape. Streaks of light blazed across the sky as helijets came and went from the estates around them. Other heejees circled down to Marica's rooftop helipad. He noticed a large one land, which looked like a Greek temple from its holos.

The doors opened with a hiss. Cris moved to the doorway and hesitated there. The night seemed singularly uninviting. He had a sudden sense of foreboding and knew deep inside that he didn't want to join the party.

Marica gave his shoulder a squeeze. "Excited?"

"I don't know."

"I have a surprise for you inside."

That piqued his interest. "Oh?"

"Come on!" She darted out, onto the tennis court, and headed toward the house down a path lined with tiny, twinkling blue lights.

Cris wondered, as he followed after the glitterfolk, if Marica's surprise had something to do with the little card she'd lost at his gallery opening. What had it said? He took it out and strained to read it again in the dim light: PACIFICA.

As the glitters poured through the open double-doors into the house, Cris found himself hanging back. Did he really want to go in? Did he really need her surprise? Did he really want to get involved with Marica again?

Jade Moon took his arm suddenly and propelled him inside. "You should dance," she said.

"I don't like to dance."

Laughing, she twirled once around him, tugging on his hands, trying to get him to join her.

"Excuse me," Cris said, "but I don't feel well."

He broke free, watched the dancers for a few moments, and then made his way back outside, thinking, *This really was a mistake. I should have known better.* Perhaps he could get one of the small heejees to take him to the city. He certainly didn't feel like staying.

The lawn was quiet. The big helijet sat desolately on the tennis court, a hulking black raven-shape, looking smaller than he'd originally thought now that its holos had been turned off. A half-dozen other heejees sat on the grass around it. Their owners were probably partying inside; he couldn't just take one.

Slowly he turned, breathing in the cool night air, surrounded by the sweet, earthy smells of growing things from flower gardens to his left and right. Marica was lucky to be on the east coast, he thought, since she liked flowers so much. The drought hadn't hit here. If anything there had been much too much rain, and tonight's dryness was a welcome change.

He stood there for a small eternity, then finally wandered into the rose garden, staring at everything around him with an artist's eye. This felt like a night straight out of his childhood, with the moon full and the sky filled with stars, before unseasonal storms and droughts that lasted years became the norm. Back then scientists had only speculated about the Greenhouse Effect instead of measuring its boundaries. During the last thirty years the world's climate had altered enough so that no one speculated any more—they knew.

Caught up in the moment, thinking of the past, Cris at first didn't notice the petite woman standing alone on the other side of the waist-high rosebush hedge, watching the moon. When he did notice, it took him a moment to recognize her: *Marica.*

She didn't seem the same glittery, darting creature who'd invaded the gallery show earlier that evening. She'd changed her makeup and clothes. Her face, no longer covered by a glaze of color, looked totally different.

Silhouetted against the main house's lights, gazing out a the pale stars and moon, she appeared sad, almost forlorn. He watched her silently for awhile, wondering if he should speak to her, or perhaps just leave.

He still felt terribly drawn to her, even more than before. She seemed so vulnerable. Almost like that first day when he had first met her at the Museum of Modern Art. She'd stood in front of his holographic 'Portrait of a Rose,' simply staring at it for the longest time. He'd watched her then as he watched her now—not knowing whether minutes had passed or hours. He'd loved her the moment he'd seen her. Too bad he hadn't known more before he'd fallen so helplessly in love.

Cris decided to get away while he could and started back toward the heejees.

"Don't go," Marica called in a trembling voice. "Cris — "

"What's wrong?" he demanded. He swallowed, then turned and moved around the hedge to join her. Tears glistened on her pale cheeks. More tears welled in her eyes.

"You never know who is going to betray you. You can't trust anyone, not friends, not family . . . ." Her voice trailed off, and suddenly she smiled. It was as though a mask had dropped into place. Now that she had an audience, he thought, she'd slipped back into performance mode.

Once before, during the first week of their honeymoon in Free Nova Scotia, he'd seen her almost open up to him. At the last minute she'd pulled away, raising all her defenses. Like now. Something had hurt her, he'd decided then, and hurt her so much that she'd run away to a little-girl play world, and she'd had the money to make it real. The glitterfolk, all her shallow trappings—there had to be a reason. He doubted she'd ever tell him what it was though.

She leaned her head against his shoulder. Softly, he stroked her hair. Her face seemed so young, so innocent, without the bizarre skin paints. Yet her eyes held the wisdom of the world. Hers was a face he never seemed to quite capture on canvas or holo, no matter how he tried. The one in the gallery tonight came the closest, but it still missed some essential inner fire. Hers was a face that always seemed new to him. It was a face of youth and hope, sadness and joy; a face that needed infinite amounts of love but could never give any in return.

He bent towards her, to kiss her. His arms wrapped around her. He knew it was wrong to let Marica get so close to him again, but he couldn't help it. He still loved her, despite the way she had treated him. He thought perhaps he always would.

She pulled away. "Please, Cris."

"Would you like to go to my studio?" he asked, knowing even as he did what her answer would be.

Abruptly, she turned and ran back toward the house. She flung open the doors and plunged into the crowd of glitterfolk, and they surged around her. She was one of them again, twisting and twirling, swaying to the music, one fluttering body indistinguishable from all the others around her. And then she was gone, lost completely.

Cris turned away, hating them all, never wanting to see any of them again. But he couldn't push Marica from his thoughts no matter how he tried. He bit his lip so hard he tasted blood. And reluctantly he turned back and headed for the dancing throng, trying to follow her.

*　　*　　*

A.J. Beaumont was still fuming two hours after the party had started. Marica and her glitter friends had shown up with astonishing abruptness, and the mansion had instantly come alive, turning into a moving, swirling torrent of people, sounds, and images. Marica had barely stopped to kiss him hello before disappearing into the crowd. After awhile he'd tried to look for her, only to be told she'd gone off for a walk in the gardens with one of her ex-husbands, an apelike holo-artist whose creations were all the latest rage.

A.J. had hardly expected Marica to be faithful, but he'd at least thought she'd spend the evening with him. After all, it had been her idea to hold this party in his honor.

He snorted. Some honor. Most of the glitterfolk studiously ignored him. And the few that did stop to talk all wanted money. They yammered about business deals, contributions to pet charities, or work for them or their relatives. Parasites, all of them. If it weren't for Marica, he would have had his bodyguards throw the lot out into the street.

A.J. glanced at his watch and decided to give Marica another fifteen minutes before he left. He'd just about had it with her. Even though he needed her shipping lines to complete the Pacifica deal, were they really worth the effort—and annoyance? He could make Pacifica work without Marica Vonn-

Grendel; it would just take a year or so longer.

He began to pace angrily, bodyguards trying to keep up while remaining unobtrusive. A.J. had built so many plans around Marica and her shipping company, he hated to have wasted the effort.

Suddenly Marica stood in front of him, appearing as if by magic from a crowd of glitterfolk. Her startling good looks made her stand out, even among the beautiful people. Her innocent yet radiant face, her body sensual as a seductress, her skimpy holodress accentuating what it didn't reveal.

Before he could react, she flung her arms around his neck and kissed him hungrily. Still angry, A.J. stood unmoved for a moment, then gave in and kissed her back just as passionately. He'd always been good at lovemaking, he told himself.

When he tried to pull away, though, Marica aggressively rubbed up against his body. Her hands slid down to brush his chest, his stomach, and then his thighs. Her kiss became deeper — her tongue and lips massaging his in an urgent rhythm. He found himself responding almost before he realized it. Slipping his arms around her, he stroked her through the flimsy fabric and down along the flesh revealed by the low-cut back. He wanted to rip through it to touch the rest.

Finally they drew apart, both gasping for breath, both laughing. For a moment, A.J. thought, the world had narrowed down to just the two of them. Marica had quite a knack for catching him off-guard; this was the second time she'd done it tonight. He didn't like that. Softly she began to kiss his chest.

A.J. became aware of someone watching them. He looked up and found Marica's ex-husband, Cristopher Morrisey, standing an arm's length away, staring. While he and A.J. were both large men, there was little other similarity between them. A.J. oozed style and elegance, from his silk suit to his slender, mani- cured hands to his fashionably styled hair. The image fit him. Though Cris still had on a tuxedo from his gallery opening, he wore it like a painter's smock. He seemed somehow hunched up inside it, A.J. thought, like an ape in human drag.

Morrisey's chestnut hair hung in an uncombed shag, and his eyes were narrowed to slits beneath heavy eyebrows. His face flushed with anger as he glared from Marica to A.J. and back again. He looked ready to kill.

"Marica, we really don't need an audience." A.J. pulled her hands away. She pouted as he broke her hold, like a selfish little girl whose candy had been taken away. Her childish expression made him smile. *It's so easy to use the greedy,* he thought.

Then Marica caught sight of Cristopher, and a flash of embarrassment crossed her face—just as quickly hidden.

So she hadn't known Morrisey had been standing there, A.J. thought. That at least was good. Her show of affection had probably been real. But her reaction—embarrassment at being caught kissing him—troubled A.J. Was she still interested in Morrisey? He was obviously still interested in her. All of which made A.J. wonder where he stood. He was used to controlling the situation as much with women as with business. And for the sake of his business it was even more important than usual that he control Marica — he certainly couldn't afford to have it the other way around.

"Is this the surprise you wanted to show me?" Cris demanded, his eyes never leaving Marica.

"Surprise?" A.J. asked, trying to sound unconcerned. He tried to pry Marica away from his body, but she clung to him persistently. "I don't know what you're talking about."

"Cris—" Marica whispered. Then she smiled regally and pulled A.J. forward. "A.J., I'd like you to meet Cristopher Morrisey, *one* of my ex-husbands. He's a very famous holographic artist, you know. He has a large exhibit in the 52nd Street Gallery right now. There's even a portrait of *me* on display. You really ought to buy it. You'd love it—I'm nude!" She laughed the hollow, carefree laugh of the glitterfolk, and there was no way of knowing if it was borne of years of practice, or something more.

"Pleased to meet you," A.J. muttered. He offered Morrisey his hand.

"And Cris, this is Alexander James Beaumont—the multi-multi-billionaire. I'm sure he's a patron of the arts. Perhaps you can get him to commission another portrait of me. Cris is dying to paint another portrait of me, you know, A.J. He thinks I have fascinating eyes." She paused to blink several times for effect. "And he is absolutely right — don't you think so?"

"Certainly," A.J. murmured. Marica's eyes were indeed stunning, and he was beginning to feel a little possessive about them right now, even though he didn't want to.

Cris shook hands, but continued to glare. A.J. shifted uncomfortably, glad his bodyguards were present in case of trouble. They could take Morrisey down in seconds flat, A.J. knew. All it took was a nod of his head.

Marica laughed again, and the circle of glitterfolk who'd gathered to watch the confrontation laughed too.

Morrisey was obviously less than entertained. His face grew less red—an improvement, A.J. thought, but not much of one. There seemed to be an undercurrent of violence in his every motion.

"I've got something to tell you, Cris," said Marica softly. Then she turned to the crowd, raised her slim arms above her head, and waved them toward her. "I've got something to tell everyone," she called out. "I've got an announcement . . . an announcement everyone!"

The glitterfolk shushed one another and surged forward to hear. The glaze-rock shut off. Silence fell.

"I'd like to announce my engagement—" she paused dramatically and looked at A.J—"to Alexander James Beaumont!"

A.J.'s mouth twitched slightly. Perhaps Marica wasn't all that predictable after all. He had been sure she would accept his proposal tonight; at least he'd been sure until he'd seen her look at Morrisey the way she had, but he had expected her to tell him privately and leave it up to him to make the announcement.

Then he grinned. What did a few minor details matter anyway, as long as it all worked out as planned. With their engagement, he'd tied up biggest deal in his life—if not all history. When Pacifica went into operation, success was certain. Marica's shipping empire completed his plans.

All the glitterfolk pressed forward, congratulating everyone in sight, a wave of human flesh and rippling holo-clothes, practically drowning Marica and A.J. with attention. Then the tide washed out as quickly as it began, as guests streamed to other parts of the house. The music surged up, louder than ever, wild with rhythmic African drumbeats. The glitterfolk began to dance, leaving Marica, Cris, and A.J. standing like an island in the center of the room.

"You could have told me earlier," said Cristopher, in an oddly strangled voice.

Marica smiled. "I didn't know I was going to accept A.J.'s sweet proposal. I hadn't made up my mind until just this minute."

She glided to A.J., slipped her arm around his waist, and clung to him.

Cris said, "I think I'd better be going now." He looked away, shuffling his feet. "I've had enough."

"Nonsense, Cris, you can't go yet. I have this wonderful idea to discuss with you and A.J. I think we can all help one another."

A.J.'s eyebrows raised. What was Marica up to now? Her having ideas was not a hopeful sign.

She went on, "I think A.J. should hire you."

"A portrait?" Cris asked doubtfully.

"No, not that." She laughed. "I thought you could help out with Pacifica." She turned to A.J. "Don't you think Cristopher could do some wonderful holograms of the island for publicity? And I'll bet he could paint a whole wall in the lobby of the reception plaza. Oh, there are all sorts of things he could do, and he's so famous he could surely help us get the project up and running, don't you think so, A.J.?" She tittered again, her childish giggle beginning to grate on A.J.'s nerves. "Sort of keep things all in the family, you know."

A.J. frowned, more annoyed at himself for not anticipating that Marica might suggest hiring Morrisey than at the suggestion itself. She'd already asked him to find work for several of her friends, so why not for the neanderthal artist? And most annoying of all, the idea was actually rather good.

Cristopher Morrisey had an international reputation as a holo-artist. He'd started out doing flowers and animals, and the ecology crowd went crazy over his work. The Green Agers particularly championed him, and he'd done the green planet holo that was their symbol.

A.J. didn't put any faith in the opinions of semi-religious, semi-ecological groups like the Green Agers, but he respected the power they controlled. The climate changes wrought by the Greenhouse Effect had made various ecology groups of the last thirty years into a major political factor. First the Greens had emerged as a political party in Europe and Canada, and eventually they'd spread to the U.S. and around the world. The Green Agers had taken up their cause and had spawned their own organized religion that merged mysticism and Christian evangelism with concerns for the environment. The Church of the Green Age had become an important religious and political force.

Pacifica's public facade would appeal to Green Agers and various other ecology-oriented groups, A.J. knew. Their support of Morrisey made him the almostperfect corporate artist for Pacifica. He would loan the project legitimacy. He would have been the perfect choice if A.J. had thought of the idea himself.

A.J. wondered whether Marica really cared about Pacifica or if she were merely trying to help her ex-husband. Was it coincidence that she'd had come up with such an intriguing idea? It didn't seem possible that under her glitter facade lay an actual mind. A.J. ran his fingers gently down Marica's firm rump, and took another look at her smooth, little-girl features. No, he decided. It just wasn't possible.

Cristopher scratched his unkempt hair absently. He looked surprised at Marica's suggestion, and faintly confused. *Dumb as an ape, too,* A.J. couldn't help but think. He found it hard to believe Cris was an artist, let alone a successful one.

"Well A.J., what do you think about my idea?" asked Marica, as she squirmed deliciously against him.

"It has some possibilities."

"Oh, A.J., I know you'll love it if you think about it."

"I'm not so sure *I* love it," interrupted Morrisey. "I'll have to think about working for Beaumont. He doesn't have the greatest record as far as environmental protection and human rights are concerned—you should know that, Marica. You have enough Green Age friends, and they're always picketing him for something."

A.J. smiled. "All that's about to change. This project can save the world."

Morrisey looked at him skeptically. "And I have plenty of other work to do, you know. I'm pretty busy. I can't drop everything for you anymore, Marica."

"You're not really all that busy, Cris," she said. "Besides, Pacifica is perfect for you. I know you want to do your bit and help the world and all that. You simply *have* to do it."

"I don't *have* to do anything!" Morrisey snarled.

Marica stared earnestly at the hulking artist. "This project is important. It can feed millions."

A.J. shrugged. "If he doesn't want to do it, that's up to him. And there are other things to consider."

Marica said, "A.J. will pay you quite handsomely."

"That's of no importance. I have more clients than I can handle already. But I'm willing to hear you out, Beaumont, since Marica seems to think this thing is so worthwhile. If you are interested in talking to me, give me a call tomorrow. I'm going home now." The big ape glanced around awkwardly. "If I can just find a ride back to the city . . ."

"Take my heejee, if you want," A.J. offered. He made a sudden decision: He wanted to use Morrisey's art to promote Pacifica. It felt like a good move, and he'd always been one to trust his instincts. "My pilot will take you home and bring you back to my shipboard office tomorrow morning. We can discuss the project further then."

"All right. But won't you need your heejee?"

"I'll be staying here tonight."

"Of course." Morrisey glared at him. "I think I can find my own way home, though."

"Nonsense," said Marica. "It's a great idea. After all, you came here in one of my heejees. You might as well take him up on his offer—he can afford it." She giggled again.

The artist gave in. "Sure, why not. Let A.J. pay for the fuel."

He took a step toward the elevator and stopped.

"There's one thing I'd like to know though." Morrisey reached into his breast pocket, took out a small white card, and tossed it to A.J.

"What *is* Pacifica?"

FOUR

JILL WASHINGTON sat half-dozing in her heejee. The party had been going on for hours now, and except for a couple of trips inside to use the toilet or grab a quick bite to eat from the kitchen, she'd remained on the roof waiting like a good little chauffeur for A.J. Beaumont's return. So much for her hopes of getting home before midnight.

At first she'd listened to newscasts on the heejee's television—but all the murders and robberies in New York, all the starving millions overseas, only depressed her further. She heard the same things every night. Bored, she finally shut the TV off.

She squirmed fitfully against the plush upholstery of the pilot's chair, which had grown uncomfortable over the long wait.

Someone tapped on the window of the heejee.

Instantly Jill snapped to full attention, coming alert with a wide-eyed look on her face that would fool one into believing she'd never dozed, a trick she'd learned in the Air Force which had proved a useful talent when working under demanding corporate executives.

She expected to see A.J. Beaumont, but instead an all-too-familiar green faced pressed against the glass. She tensed. *Jade Moon.*

"Go away," she mouthed silently. Hands sweaty, Jill found herself gripping the arms of her seat.

Jade Moon tapped again, persistently. She kept tapping even when Jill shook her head no.

She's not going to leave me alone. I might as well get it over with.

Jill opened the heejee's door and slid out. "I gave you my answer yesterday," she said, voice a bit too strident. "We have nothing further to discuss."

"Hear me out." Jade Moon smiled, and her teeth were as green as her face. "Come." She started walking toward the shadows, then turned and waited patiently.

Jill glanced around, self-conscious, her anxiety building. She shouldn't worry, she told herself. No one would think it unusual for her to talk to one of Marica Vonn-Grendel's best friends.

But as she followed Jade Moon to the darkest part of the roof near the strange, guardian mannequins, Jill kept her eyes on the gargoyle holo concealing the elevator doors. If Beaumont came back, she'd be ready, she told herself.

Jade Moon smiled again. "I thought you might need more time to think about our offer. We know how you feel. The Church can help you."

"I told you, I'm not interested."

"Look out there." Jade Moon gave an expansive wave that took in the flower gardens, the tennis courts, the stables and servants quarters, the neatly trimmed acres of grassy lawn. "The Green Age is coming, when there will be plenty for all. Those who help make our dreams reality will reap the bounty."

"Like anyone who can afford an expensive estate, you mean."

"The Green Age is coming for all, not just the rich."

Jill snorted. "And if I don't help you, I lose my chance at Paradise, is that it? I liked your bribery attempt better. I don't believe in all that crystal pseudo-science nonsense of yours."

"As is your right," Jade Moon said, with a slight nod. "However . . . we know you could use the money. Your parents could lose their house and farm soon, despite the checks you send them each month."

"How could you know that?" Jill demanded, startled.

Jade shrugged. "It's easy to check with banks. And the legal processes involved are all public." She pulled a couple of folded papers from some hidden pocket and handed them to Jill. "See for yourself."

Jill scanned the pages. Most were photocopies from newspapers like the *County Tribune*. The Sheriff's office had filed notices about her parents' delinquent real estate taxes.

Angrily, Jill crumpled the pages. Then she turned away, breathing hard. *Damn the woman!* Jade Moon had no business prying into her parents' affairs. Jill already knew about the lien. She'd hoped to save enough from her regular job to eventually settle the debt. Still, it had become a struggle to help with her parent's mortgage, their taxes, and her two older sisters' families. Showing her the papers was like plunging a knife into an open wound.

Jade Moon's honey-smooth voice explained, "The Green Age works toward the greatest good." She touched Jill's arm gently. "Believe me, the midwest will bloom again, but it will take many years. More pressing matters concern us today—like feeding the world's hungry. Pacifica is part of the answer. Beaumont plans to use Pacifica to seize economic control of the world. The Pacifica technology must be shared, not kept secret for the benefit of one greedy man."

Pacifica—that word was a magic phrase around Beaumont Industries, Jill knew. The boss's pet project, very hush-hush even in the corporate offices, was rumored to be A.J.'s newest license to print money.

Jill stubbornly shook her head. She didn't want to get sucked into this mess. It wasn't fair. All she'd ever wanted was a safe, quiet life for herself and her family. But how could they have that life anymore with famine, energy shortages, rioting, and the likelihood that her parents could soon lose their farm?

"I don't even know what Pacifica *is*," she said. "How could I help you?"

Jade Moon didn't seem to hear. She opened her emerald-sequined purse and pulled out an envelope. "One hundred thousand dollars, plus we'll give you a regular monthly salary . . . enough to pay all your parents' bills, enough to help your other relatives. Take it, Jill, you need it. All you have to do is keep your eyes open for us. Anything you can find out about Pacifica will be of interest."

So much money . . .

If Pacifica would make Beaumont even richer while the rest of the world suffered, why shouldn't she help Jade and the Green Agers? Why should her family live in poverty and despair? Wouldn't it be best if the world shared Pacifica's technology—whatever it was? She felt torn and ashamed for being tempted.

Jade Moon thrust the envelope into her hands, and Jill took it automatically. She thought of Judas, the betrayer, but Beaumont was more like Pontius Pilate than Christ.

Smiling sweetly, Jade Moon said, "You *are* going to be helping the whole world." Then she turned and walked quickly across the rooftop, back to the party.

Jill considered throwing the envelope at Jade Moon's retreating figure, but thought better of it. *I've gone too far for that now,* she thought. It had probably been too late the moment she failed to tell Beaumont about Jade Moon and the Green Agers.

She took a deep breath. The night air tasted rich and moist, full of promise. The stars overhead glittered brightly. She'd made her decision, and she'd stick with it. Hopefully she'd made the right one.

Slowly, she stuck the envelope into the secret money compartment of her belt pouch. She'd count it later, though she knew Jade Moon wouldn't cheat her on the first bribe. She wondered if she should take it to a bank, but such a large deposit might be traceable. Perhaps it would be better to buy money orders and use them to pay bills. The money would save her parents' home and make life so much easier for her impoverished sisters and their families.

Sighing, she returned to her heejee. Before she closed the door, she saw the elevator open. A figure stood silhouetted for a moment before stepping onto the roof.

At first Jill thought Jade Moon had come back, but as the form approached she realized it was a man, a stranger wearing a slightly rumpled, black tuxedo. His thick, wild mane cascaded to his shoulders—hair totally out of fashion in either the world of the dyed and sculpted glitterfolk or of the more prosaically short-haired working class which struggled just to survive.

The man reached Jill's heejee and leaned inside the cabin. "Is this one Beaumont's?"

"Of course." Jill waved casually to the heejee's tail, where the words 'Beaumont Industries' were painted. She knew the man could not have heard her conversation with Jade Moon, but despite her best efforts a guilty flush crept up her face.

"Ah, I didn't notice . . ." Distractedly, he kept glancing at the gargoyle-shaped elevator. He took a step back toward the party, hesitated, then turned to her again. "Beaumont said you'd take me into the city."

Now that he faced her directly, Jill realized he looked familiar. As tall as Beaumont, he had a wide and appealing face—high forehead, blue-green eyes, a broad nose that might have been broken once, and thick lips framed with the crinkles of laugh-lines. From the stubble on his cheeks, he hadn't shaved in a couple of days.

"Mr. Beaumont said you could use his heejee?" she asked doubtfully. That didn't sound like her boss.

"Yes, he's staying here for the night and said you could fly me home." An odd look of pain crossed the man's face as he spoke. "Why don't you check with him?"

"I'll do that."

She closed the heejee's door, slipped on her headset, and flicked on the radio. One of Marica Vonn-Grendel's servants answered.

"May I please speak to Mr. Beaumont?" Jill asked. Her fingers fidgeted with her belt pouch's zipper. "I need to know whether he authorized someone else to use the corporate heejee tonight."

Putting her on hold, the servant went to find A.J.

While she waited, Jill studied the big man with a measuring glance. Who was he? Obviously depressed, he leaned against the heejee, watching the mansion glumly. His shoulders slumped forward. Jill still couldn't shake the feeling that she knew him, which was odd since his long hair, starting to go naturally gray, would make him stand out in any crowd.

Alexander Beaumont's voice finally crackled over the headset's radio: "Yes, what is it?" His annoyance was obvious.

"Excuse me, sir, I'm sorry to interrupt, but there's a man at your heejee who said you'd authorized him to use it."

"Oh, sure." Beaumont's voice lost some of its hostility. "Cristopher Morrisey. Take him anywhere he wants. Stay available to him, and tomorrow afternoon pick him up and bring him to the *Lady Pecunia*. He's going to be working for me. I'll use one of the Vonn-Grendel heejees to get back."

"Cristopher Morrisey?" The name struck a chord in her, like the man's face.

"Yeah. He's a pain in the ass, but be nice to him."

"Yes, sir."

"Goodnight, Washington," said Beaumont, disconnecting.

Yes, sir, Jill thought silently. *Anything you want, sir.* Now she had to ferry this bozo Morrisey around all night, and God only knew when she'd get back to her apartment. *Damn all businessmen,* she thought, *and their business deals.* She began to feel a little less guilty about agreeing to spy on Beaumont.

33

She opened the heejee's door. "Please get in, Mr. Morrisey." She coated her words with enough politeness to hide her annoyance completely. "Mr. Beaumont says I should take you wherever you wish."

Morrisey sighed, took a last longing look at the elevators, and climbed into the heejee. Like Beaumont, he chose to sit beside her. He slammed the door.

"Excuse me sir, but do I know you?" asked Jill. "You look so familiar, but . . ."

He turned and gazed at her, really seeing her for the first time. His eyes flicked across her long braided hair, light chocolate skin, high cheekbones, and thin patrician nose. His eyes were very intense.

"No, I don't think so," he said. "You've probably seen my picture on the tube or in the papers. I'm an artist, and my work's gotten quite a bit of air-play recently."

Jill nodded slowly, realizing she had heard of the holo-artist before, but still not convinced she hadn't also met him in person somewhere.

"I'm Jill Washington."

"Cris Morrisey. Pleased to meet you."

"Where to, sir?"

"Ah—" Morrisey still seemed distraught. "Back to New York City, 190th and Overlook Terrace. That's where I have my studio . . . my apartment."

"Yes, sir." She'd been expecting Greenwich Village or Park Avenue, not an uptown address near The Cloisters. She shrugged—none of her business.

Punching the coordinates into the heejee's computer, she ran a quick series of safety checks. They lifted off, heading south toward the city. Morrisey twisted around to watch the Vonn-Grendel estate until its lights vanished in the distance. Then he turned around and looked at her.

"Have you worked for Beaumont Industries long?" He asked.

"Just a couple of months."

"Do you know anything about Pacifica?"

"Not really," she replied. "But I'm not allowed to talk about company projects with outsiders anyway, so I couldn't tell you anything even if I *did* know." *And I guess that makes me one of the biggest hypocrites of all time,* she thought. "Why do you ask?"

"Beaumont offered me a job doing the promotional art for his Pacifica project, but I don't know anything about it. I can't accept the position without more information. He wouldn't tell me anything tonight, except that Pacifica's going to save the world. It's intriguing—but frustrating, too, to say the least."

"It's supposed to be quite large, that's all I know," Jill said. That much had to be true.

Morrisey gazed out the window, brooding about something. "I wouldn't have thought of Beaumont as a humanitarian."

A.J. Beaumont a humanitarian? Jill smiled.

They reached New York City's airspace, and City Control took over piloting the heejee. They angled down, merging with more crowded traffic lanes, and slowed to a near crawl.

Morrisey grinned suddenly. He had an engaging smile, Jill thought. Relaxed, his face looked different, more intelligent and sensitive.

"Beaumont isn't the kind of guy to save the world for the hell of it," he said, "is he?"

Jill shrugged, thinking of her bargain with Jade Moon. "I really couldn't say, sir. I've only worked for his company for a couple of months. Perhaps Mr. Beaumont needs some good publicity, so he's sponsoring this Pacifica thing. Who knows?"

"Perhaps," Morrisey mused. "Or maybe he's just trying to impress Marica Vonn-Grendel." Cris's hands clenched and unclenched. "She's always into fads, and she has enough Green Age friends . . . with the drought and all, saving the environment must be one of her pet projects, too." He gave a short bark of laughter. "She should meet the Green Age's head bishop. What a bunch of phonies! If they actually solved the world's pollution problems and reversed the Greenhouse Effect, they wouldn't have any more converts, or their money. Oh, sorry—my apologies if you're a member. Sometimes I talk too much."

"That's okay. I don't believe all that Green Age bullshit, either." Jill felt a relieved; Morrisey clearly had nothing to do with Jade Moon or the Green Agers.

They reached the Harlem River and circled over a sea of skyscrapers. Heejee landing pads sprouted from their roofs like giant mushrooms. Personal heejees had become quite popular after automobiles were banned from Manhattan more than a dozen years ago. There was talk that they would soon ban the heejees too, since the air traffic problems had become tremendous. Within minutes they reached 190th Street.

"Where do you want me to land, sir?" Jill switched to manual control.

"My building's on the corner, the tall one with the view of the park. I don't have a helipad on the roof, but you can use Overlook Terrace. That's it there," he said, pointing.

Land on the street, thought Jill, *in a residential area?* Still, Morrisey doubtless knew about his own neighborhood's safety.

Shrugging, she switched on the spotlights lining her heejee's underside and did as instructed. She brought them down next to the rocky cliff that marked the edge of Fort Tryon Park, on cracked, weed-filled asphalt. With the auto traffic ban, everyone made deliveries by heejee, so most roads had become giant sidewalks, heejee parking lots, or free garbage dumps.

The heejee's underside spotlights didn't provide all that much illumination on the ground; the darkness around them seemed oppressive. Jill peered into the shadows doubtfully. She still remembered the good old days of cheap power and missed the security public streetlights offered.

"Nice landing," Morrisey said. "The crosswinds can be tricky alongside the cliff. You landed in minimum time and with good fuel conservation."

She looked at him sharply—and suddenly remembered how she knew him. "You were an instructor in one of my classes at Colorado Springs," she said, half-accusingly.

Cris nodded.

"It was my first year there," Jill continued. "Just for a month or so, then you left the Academy."

"And the Air Force," he added.

"You looked different then." And she couldn't help blurting out: "God your hair is long now!"

He laughed. "Not regulation anymore, huh? That was a lifetime ago."

"But what happened? Air Force pilots don't usually turn into world-famous artists."

"I left that part of my life behind. When I entered the service I was a kid, naive enough to think I could help the world somehow. I didn't expect the things I found . . . sometimes, I guess things just change, or people do." He unstrapped himself. "Well, thanks for the ride, Washington. Good flying."

As he opened the heejee's door with his right hand, he gave her a half-hearted salute with his left. Chuckling, he hopped to the ground.

At that moment, two men darted around from the back of the heejee. They'd been sitting too long, chatting, giving the men time to get close.

Morrisey yelled and twisted as one man swung a baseball bat. It caught him in the shoulders, spinning him around. The other began to pound his back with bare fists.

With a sudden sick jolt of horror, Jill realized she'd been too interested in Morrisey to pay attention to the monitors.

Jill didn't think about her own danger as she automatically punched on the heejee's rooftop spotlights, hoping to scare the attackers off. Flaring to life, they illuminated seven or eight figures on the street corner. A few men hovered a safe distance from the heejee, watching and waiting, but too afraid of the heejee's defense systems to come any closer. However, Jill couldn't activate the weapons with Morrisey so close—the machine-gun fire would rip him apart.

Morrisey had one of the muggers in a stranglehold. As they tumbled out of view she saw the bat smash into his arm.

Reaching under the dash, she pulled out the 9mm automatic she'd been issued by Beaumont Industries. She'd checked it herself recently, since Beaumont, ever paranoid, had insisted she show it to him, unload and load it, take it apart and clean it, all to prove she could handle firearms.

Locking her door so she couldn't be taken from behind, she climbed across to Morrisey's seat. The door stood open; she slid out cautiously.

As her feet hit the broken pavement, someone tackled her from the side. She whirled, glimpsing a pale, pimply face.

Jill's hand whipped around and she fired automatically. The teenager jerked backwards like a puppet on a string, blood spraying from the gaping wound in his chest. The knife he'd held went flying. He hit ground and didn't move.

Jill took a half-second to scan the area around her, spotting several of the watchers backing away into the shadows.

Morrisey and the muggers fought near the heejee's tail. Three men now attacked him.

One of the men stopped to gape at her—he couldn't have been more than seventeen or eighteen. Another brought his club down toward Morrisey's head. Jill set her feet and aimed with more care, firing calmly and precisely.

The bullet nicked his arm. Yelping, he dropped the bat, turned, and fled into the darkness, leaving a trail of blood.

Just then a volley of rifle shots rang out around her. Jill dived back to the fuselage for cover. Her face dripped with sweat, and she could almost smell her own fear. The ragged sound of her breathing seemed almost as loud as the gunfire.

Some of the shots hit the heejee's roof, breaking solar cells. *There's going to be hell to pay when Beaumont sees this*, she thought. Then she wondered why she was wasting what could very well be the last moments of her life thinking about A.J. Beaumont.

Morrisey still fought with two men, a slender teen and a larger, slightly older man. Wedged too far under the heejee to get a good shot, especially with Morrisey in the way, Jill didn't dare fire.

Ignoring the scattered bullets that continued to hit the ground in the open in front of her, Jill rolled out, firing into the darkness beyond the heejee's spotlights, aiming at the unseen marksman who seemed to be behind some parked cars at the end of the street. Silence answered instead of return fire, so she must have hit someone. She reacted automatically now, thinking of the muggers as targets rather than human beings.

As she staggered to her feet, the larger man pulled away from Morrisey and ran toward her. She fired awkwardly, missed, and started to take aim again. Whirling, the man kicked out, and his toe connected with her arm with karate force, almost knocking the gun from her hand.

Moving into him, Jill stomped down heavily on his right foot and jabbed into his solar plexus with her left elbow. The big man grabbed her braid, yanking her almost off her feet. With the gun still in her right hand, she swung toward his chin. It connected to his jaw with a sharp crack, breaking it. He howled and released his grip on her hair. He wobbled backward. Finally able to train her gun on him, she purposely aimed just above his head, ready to shoot lower if he came at her again. Instead he turned and lumbered toward one of the buildings across the street.

She fired another warning shot after him, and he bolted away. Morrisey's remaining attacker followed him into the shadows.

Jill felt a surge of exhilaration. She ran to Morrisey's side and helped him sit up. Blood streamed from a cut above his eyes.

"Can you stand?" she asked.

"I think so."

Jill helped him to his feet; he stood unsteadily. His face seemed unnaturally pale. She thought he might have a concussion and perhaps some broken bones.

"Let's get you back to the heejee," she said. "I'll take you to a hospital."

"No, that's okay. I've had worse . . . just got a few lumps on my head, that's all. I've got pain-killers in my apartment."

Jill glanced around apprehensively. The muggers had faded into the night, leaving behind the body of the one she'd apparently killed. Luckily the self-defense laws were liberal enough to protect her, she thought, if anyone cared enough about the man to file a complaint. It only took one witness, and Morrisey was hers. And if the dead man's friends or relatives didn't come back for the body, the sanitation department would pick it up for cremation. All very fast, neat, and efficient.

"I really think you should see a doctor."

"No, I'm all right, damn it." Morrisey shook his head stubbornly.

"Then I'll go up with you." Beaumont was going to be angry enough about her dropping Morrisey off in a dangerous area. She'd better make damn sure he got safely home. "Just hang on a minute."

She sprinted back to the heejee, grabbed her purse, another clip for her gun, and the heejee computer's remote control. Stepping down, she activated the computer's defense system and the heejee's doors closed and locked automatically behind her. Purple lights began to pulsate along the roof, warning people to stay at least ten feet away at all times. If anyone tried to break in, various weapons would come to play, ranging from electrified door-handles to bullets from the rooftop machine guns. Only the remote control with its scrambled access code—now firmly tucked into Jill's belt pouch—could deactivate the heejee's auto-defense.

"Hurry up," she told Cris, letting him lean upon her for support. "We've got about two minutes before the heejee's spotlights shut off." She didn't relish the thought of being left in darkness. On the other hand, inside the heejee's lights they could become easy rifle targets.

She led Cris toward the corner building he'd indicated earlier, scanning the area for any attackers. A few men and women up the street seemed to be studiously avoiding them—which was fine in her book. She kept her gun in view, a warning to all.

They reached Morrisey's building just as the spotlights on the heejee winked out. Cris slowly punched a long combination into the lock. The door slid aside, revealing a freight elevator.

Cris staggered inside. Jill took one last glance around, then followed. The corner seemed deserted now, the only movement the blinking purple lights on the heejee's roof.

Cris punched another code into the elevator's computer; the doors closed and the car began to rise. By the lone fluorescent bulb overhead, he looked worse than ever, his left eye dark and swelling from bruises, blood trickling down his cheek, sweat beading on his forehead. His breathing was shallow and fast, but he stood straighter now, as though drawing strength from some inner reserve.

Relieved, Jill sank back against the wall. She felt drained, almost nauseous. Back at work, her conscious mind began to race, taking her off autopilot. As it went over every little detail from the fight, she realized that she'd really killed that one young man—hardly older than a boy. *They would have killed us both if they had the chance,* she thought, but it didn't help. She still felt sick.

It had all been her fault. She should have used the rooftop spotlights. She should have checked the area before letting Cris leave the heejee. She should have been paying more attention to the outside monitors than to their conversation.

"Are you hurt?" Morrisey suddenly asked her.

"No, not a scratch." Pulling herself together, she thumbed the automatic's safety and stuck it into her belt. "How about you? You don't look too good to me. I should have insisted on taking you to the hospital."

"I think I'm all right," he replied.

"Were those guys trying to rob us, or were they your neighbors settling up some grudge?"

"They could be my neighbors, I suppose, after quick bucks from the local rich artist, or a nice, new heejee. I don't know. Gangs don't usually run in this area. It's always been very safe."

When the elevator reached the top floor, its doors opened to reveal a brick wall and another keypad. Cris punched another code, then the wall slid soundlessly aside, revealing an apartment. Dim lights came on automatically.

"Maybe we ought to call the police now," offered Jill.

"Don't bother," Morrisey said. "They're too busy preventing food riots downtown to worry about a justified shooting. That's one reason why they passed all the vigilante and self-defense laws, after all."

"I guess," she said slowly.

Morrisey went to one of the windows, pulled up the blinds, and peered out. "They've already taken the body, anyway," he said. Then he sagged wearily into one unit of the overstuffed sectional that took up most of his living room. Suddenly he winced, sucking air through his teeth. "Shit, I think they cracked a rib."

"Great." Jill sighed and bent over him. "Let me take a look." As she unbuttoned his shirt, she wondered how she'd explain all this to her boss. Delivering Morrisey safely home had been her responsibility, and somehow she didn't think Beaumont would be very understanding when he learned she'd let her package become damaged in transit.

FIVE

MARICA STUDIED her reflection in the large mirror above her dresser. She looked as pale and dull as a wilted lily, she thought, and felt about the same way. It was time to recreate herself.

She glanced over to the large, round bed where A.J. Beaumont still slept. Curled into a ball beneath her ruffled pink comforter, he looked as soft and sweet as a child.

Reaching into the ultrasonic lens-cleaner case, she extracted the dark blue lenses that transformed her eyes from pale robin's egg to alluring peacock blue. Then she began carefully applying makeup, a thin coating of foundation to smooth her skin, contour cream to heighten her cheekbones and reduce the size of her nose, a bit of blush to color her cheeks, eye liner and mascara to emphasize her eyes. She applied only the bare minimum to enhance her features; few people would guess she wore any makeup at all, yet it was enough to transform her from being merely pretty to head-turning, absolutely picture-perfect *stunning*.

Thinking back to her days in high school, she smiled wryly. She'd been so different then: mousy brown hair chopped off at ear-length, often by her own hand; shaggy eyebrows; the gawky, too big nose; the pudgy roundness of a face that ate too much.

That had been before she'd learned to recreate herself—when she'd been called Susan or Sue and lived at home with her parents. Now her long, silky hair glowed a radiant blond. Her plucked eyebrows arched elegantly. Her nose had been surgically bobbed to precisely the right length. Now she was perfect in every way.

She usually tried to forget the old days, to bury them in the deepest hole her mind could create. But every once in awhile it was almost pleasurable to remember her old face and old life, to bask in the beauty of her new one.

It had all begun the day she'd lightened her hair and started calling herself Marica. It sounded sort of like America as well as reminding her of Marcia Kincaid, the beautiful actress.

How her parents had hated it when she'd changed her name. It had seemed the worst sort of insult to them. That was probably the main reason she'd thought of it. How she had taunted them with it—announcing it to any and everyone she met, having all her friends phone the house to ask for *Marica.* She chuckled.

Of course her father hadn't objected to her new blond hair and prettier looks . . . She pushed that thought away.

They hadn't been able to stop her from calling herself Marica. It had been such a simple idea, really. It had been the first victory she had won over her parents.

A new name, a new life. That's what she'd told herself.

It all came true when Todd Benjamin got interested in her, and they'd run off and eloped at age seventeen. He'd been a millionaire, and he'd been in love. . . .

Marica looked at A.J. again. He reminded her of Todd, in a way, with that blond hair and boyish face of his. He wasn't so bad really, just like Jade Moon had said.

Her thoughts returned to Todd. *Has it really been eight years since I married him?* Who would have known he would die so soon with his parents in that heejee crash, leaving his bride of only a few months a very wealthy widow.

Todd had gotten her away from her parents. His money bought her a whole new life.

She noticed A.J. beginning to stir in his sleep. He'd be awake soon, and he'd probably he would want to have sex again, unless she could convince him that he had too much work to do. But maybe it was wiser to go back to bed with him. That would make him more docile, and she wanted to get him to take her to visit Pacifica. She'd never been there, and it seemed like a good idea to find out more about it.

Marica had never paid much attention to the Green Agers and their causes, but Jade Moon seemed quite concerned about the environment and the future of the world. She seemed to think that A.J.'s project could have major benefits for everyone.

In fact, if it hadn't been for Jade, she might never have met the busy industrialist. She remembered what Jade had said when she'd first mentioned A.J: "I dated him for a few weeks, but I got bored with him. I think he's more your type. You'd get along perfectly together. And there is one thing I did like about him, though, he's great in bed." Jade had arranged an introduction.

Marica liked Jade Moon. Her friend seemed a kindred spirit in many ways, with ambitions lurking behind her carefree facade which might be almost as strong as Marica's own. She smiled to herself. Jade had changed her name too, though for different reasons. Church members often took 'natural' names—plants, minerals, flowers, and even astronomical objects like the moon—to show their oneness with nature, the universe, and God.

Jade Moon had encouraged Marica to join the Green Age, but some of the members were too fanatical for her liking. The Green Agers had splintered into two factions several years before, with the more radical Green Action Now! group taking to the underground, from which they periodically emerged to make nuisances of themselves.

The GANs resorted to terrorism in their search for ways to stop pollution and restore the Earth's delicate ecological balance. They were the type of people who put spikes into trees so that the loggers who cut them would wreck their saws; sometimes the loggers were injured. They even bombed projects they didn't like and had once assassinated a Senator from Florida. Marica had heard rumors from some of her friends that the GANs had crept back into the Church again, but Jade Moon dismissed the idea as paranoid fantasy. "We'd never take them back," she vowed. "Their terrorism in the name of ecology did more to wreck our good name than anything our enemies could ever throw at us."

Turning back to the mirror, Marica brushed her hair outward so it cascaded down her back in rippling waves of gold. It had been so easy to capture A.J.'s attention. It seemed to be like that with all men. Ever since she was 12 years old they had swarmed around her. She'd been innocent then and afraid. . . .

She consciously pushed those memories away.

Until she met Todd, she hadn't realized she could use her sexuality to get what she wanted. When she lost him it became a game to go after men for presents and attention. Later it developed into a more sophisticated contest: which affair or marriage would give her more wealth and international attention? She married three men in quick succession after Todd, and now she owned stocks, bonds, estates, and a small empire of ships, publishing houses, and food industries.

Cris Morrisey was the only exception to the pattern, though it had been his fame that first attracted her. Then she had learned more about him and became interested for all the wrong reasons.

An idealist with a real love for people, animals, and the world around him, he was unlike anyone she'd ever known. He always seemed aware of the core of unhappiness within her that no one else seemed to notice, even though she'd never opened up and told him why. Sometimes she thought he really wanted her happiness more than his own. That was why she ended their relationship. She almost lost control over him, and over herself.

A.J. Beaumont rolled over and sat up.

Marica's lips turned upward in a cute little grin. It was a perfect performance, and A.J. never saw the Cheshire Cat in her smile. He was the fattest mouse she'd ever caught.

"Oh darling, you're awake at last." Cooing prettily, she bounced onto the bed next to him. As if by accident, the top of her skimpy baby-doll nightgown dipped, exposing most of her left breast. She bounced up and down like an excited puppy, making the most of the little girl pout the men seemed to adore. "I'm so happy."

A.J.'s gaze seemed transfixed by the sight of her nipples. She bounced again, a little harder, and the baby-doll inched up as well, showing a glimpse of inner thighs and dark golden curls.

A.J. reached for her, pulling her down on the bed. His hands caressed her eagerly. He was a good lover, thorough and gentle, trying to make her climax just as he had been told to do in all the sex manuals he'd read. But like the rest of the men she'd known, he failed miserably. And like the rest, he thought himself a wonderful lover, never suspecting her writhing body, moans, and final collapse were a charade.

When he rolled off of her, Marica curled next to him, pressing her head against his chest. She whispered, "That was wonderful. I love you so much."

Keeping quiet, she leaned against him, thinking erotic thoughts of her own. She felt more excited now than when they'd made love. She knew that asking him for more would do no good; she could tell by the regularity of his breathing, he'd already gone back to sleep.

She rose, went to the intercom, and ordered breakfast. Her servant, Adelle, promised it would be right up.

"Everything's ready, as you ordered last night."

"Good," Marica said.

Five minutes later, Adelle and Pierre wheeled two silver carts into her bedroom. The noise and the smell of strong coffee brought A.J. awake again. He quickly pulled the covers up over himself, looking a bit embarrassed to be caught naked by mere servants.

He covered it quickly enough, though. "Great idea, Marica," he said, sitting up. "How'd you know I was starving?"

"I know everything my man needs," she said, climbing back into bed next to him. She gave his thigh a squeeze through the bedspread.

Pierre set lap-trays in front of them, and they dug eagerly into their steak, cantaloupe, and pan-fried potatoes and tofu mix. Only the rich could afford such a breakfast, now that worldwide drought had reduced most people to rations of rice, soy protein, and the occasional chicken or egg.

"Do you have any special plans for the day?" she asked between bites.

"Hmmm? Not really. I should be getting back to my office, I suppose. I'm probably late for half a dozen appointments."

"I was wondering if you could set something up so that we could go to Pacifica together. I'm really anxious to see it."

"I think we could arrange it. Perhaps next week."

"Can't we go to Pacifica today? If you're going to get Cris working on the project, you'll have to show it to him. Couldn't you take me along too? You know how much I want to see it."

Pacifica—the word itself sounded romantic. A place and a process, A.J. had told her. An island where all of mankind's dreams would come true. She wondered if perhaps A.J.'s project had interested her even more than his wealth and power. Maybe she'd grown a bit bored with glitter fads and hedonistic pursuits.

Or maybe some of Cris's interests had rubbed off on her. He always complained about the state of the world, sounding off about poverty and pollution, rioting and politicians. And Jade Moon was the same way, always pushing her to use her wealth to help other people.

When A.J. talked about using the sea to save the world, it sounded appealing. She *could* help out, and it wouldn't cost her a thing. A.J. would do it all.

"At least three-quarters of the world is ocean," he'd said. "Why not use that resource to solve the food shortage?"

Aquaculture, he called it. That word sounded romantic as well.

"We can really make a name for ourselves with Pacifica," A.J. had told her. "The secret is kelp—seaweed. Red algae is gathered for food, especially in countries like Japan. Other kinds of algae serve as condiments or emulsifiers. But kelp, though plentiful, never really caught on. There are many reasons. First, most kinds don't have much protein. It's not an efficient food source. Second, it grows best on rocky shorelines, and most of those are very polluted. Hell, it's hard enough to find an edible oyster or clam anymore! And lastly, though the Japanese think it's a delicacy, most kelp tastes pretty awful."

A.J. had puffed up like a peacock with his own self-congratulation. "But my company solved the problems. We've bio-engineered a new bacteria that changes the cellulose in a species of brown kelp into starch. It is sort of like fermentation, but you don't end up with alcohol. The final mash is nutritious and neutral in taste, rather like potato. It can be dried, processed, and artificially flavored—makes a real good flour too. It can be used in breads, cakes, or as a main dish."

Marica had cooed appreciatively.

He went on, "We've also come up with a way to farm the stuff in deeper sea waters. Instead of rooting on rocks, the kelp will anchor on special net-like mylar lattices. We can put the kelp beds anywhere. And in international waters no one can tax us or try to control our production." He laughed. "Hell, the more we produce, the better the world's going to be. Our kelp will actually absorb carbon dioxide, as well as produce oxygen. It could slow down or even stop the Greenhouse Effect, once we get into full swing.

"Beaumont Industries will be bigger than General Electric, and when you marry me, you're going to be part of it all."

Power, that was certainly a motive behind A.J.'s plan. That was something with which she could identify. But the idea of stopping the riots over food, reversing the Greenhouse Effect, and ending the New Depression also had its appeal. Not only did it help other people, it satisfied some of her own more selfish needs.

If everything worked, Beaumont would go down in the history books alongside such greats as Pasteur, Edison, Salk and others who had changed the world for the better. Getting that kind of fame was a far more exciting inducement than increasing her fortune. She would be Marica Beaumont. And perhaps she could even get him to name the kelp after her.

"I suppose we can fly over to Pacifica if you want." said A.J., bringing Marica suddenly back to the present.

"Maybe we can get married there," she said. "We could have the wedding party on your yacht, and announce Pacifica at the same time. After all, you said you'd be going public about it next few weeks. Wouldn't it be grand? That is, if you want to get married so soon."

"The sooner the better, Marica. I told you that when I asked you to marry me."

She sighed sweetly. "I know, honey. But I have so much to do. I have to plan the wedding, invite all the guests, and of course do the most important thing—get a terrific gown."

A.J. rolled his eyes and flopped back on the bed with a look of exasperation.

Marica chuckled inwardly. Sometimes she had such fun playing an empty-headed bimbo. She could prattle on about clothes for hours and drive someone like A.J. absolutely nuts if she wanted to. Then she could apply a gentle nudge in the right direction, and the man would be so glad to be off of the subject of clothing he would talk to her about any subject she wanted . . . and tell her his deepest secrets without the slightest restraint.

She nuzzled the back of his hand with her lips, and took him off the hook. "But I love you so much, I just can't wait that long. I'm going to call my designer today and get him to get something ready for me."

"I suppose we could have the wedding on the yacht," mused A.J. "But I'm not sure if I'm quite ready to make Pacifica public knowledge yet. There are too many details to finish up. But I'll think about it."

"All right, darling. Just let me know. Meanwhile, I'll get started on the wedding. Your yacht is going to be just terrific!"

"Marica, please don't make it too complicated, I really would like to marry you as soon as possible."

"Don't worry, dear, my staff can whip up incredible parties at almost no notice. Jade Moon will help me too, she's great at organizing things. I'm sure they can have everything arranged by the end of next week."

"Really?" A.J. sat up abruptly. He looked quite pleased. "Are you sure you can invite everyone by then?"

"No problem."

"What about your parents? You never seem to want to talk about them. I haven't met them yet, and I probably should. After all, we *are* getting married."

Marica's usual composure slipped for an instant. "I'm not inviting them, and don't you *dare,* either. They don't care what happens to me, and I prefer it that way."

"Are you sure?" asked Beaumont, looking puzzled.

Marica forced herself to laugh lightly, as though it hardly mattered to her. "Don't worry about them—they are *so* boring anyway. You're lucky you won't have to meet them." She swallowed. "Besides, I want our wedding to be something really *special.* Maybe Cris will paint a wedding portrait of us? Or do you think he is going to be too busy with Pacifica?"

"Oh yeah, Morrisey," said A.J. thoughtfully. "He was going to meet me on the *Lady Pecunia* today. I suppose I can have my pilot bring him to the airport instead. You're right, he needs to see Pacifica." He got a puppy-dog look on his face and snuggled up against her. "But I'd rather just take you."

"Don't be jealous darling, it's just good business sense to get use Cris as our artist."

"I know, I know," he said. "We went through all that yesterday, and you're right." He extricated himself from her cuddles, stood, and stretched. His lean body was tanned and fit, Marica saw. He was almost too picture-perfect, she thought, like his smile.

He patted Marica's head like a doting father.

"Get DiNucci to design your wedding dress. He's the best, and he can be fast if you pay him enough. Bill it to my company."

"Oh, sweetie, that's a *fabulous* idea." Marica giggled softly. DiNucci was the world's most famous designer. She'd be getting an extravagantly expensive gown on top of everything else. Mentally, she tripled the yacht-party's budget. With a DiNucci gown, you *really* had to celebrate. And she'd have it all thanks to Alexander James Beaumont.

Her wedding would be the bash of the decade. Everyone invited would be suitably grateful—she'd make sure of it.

Smoothing her nightgown, she stretched out languidly, watching A.J. dress. It was all working out even better than she'd dared to hope.

SIX

A shrill trilling roused Cris halfway out of his sleep. He didn't want to wake up. He felt like he'd been through a hamburger grinder, and every movement brought fresh meaning to the word *pain*. His right shoulder ached the worst, a sharp throbbing to the rhythm of his heartbeat.

Moaning, he stumbled from bed and headed for the bathroom. He reached for the mini-blinds, but everything seemed to be in the wrong place. Confused, he rubbed the sleep from his eyes, realized he was turned around, and reoriented himself. The universe sat a little further to the right than he'd thought. He found the rod connected to the mini-blinds, turned it, and flooded the room the sunlight.

The sudden glare hurt his eyes, but he was used to that; you didn't use electric lights during the day if you had windows. Yawning, he scrunched open his eyes and stared into the mirror. Ugly bruises ran along the right side of his jaw. Blood stained the large bandage on his forehead. He touched it and winced; they'd certainly gotten him last night.

His pajama top had each button one step out of place. As he rebuttoned it, he discovered that his ribs had been taped. He vaguely remembered Jill Washington doing it the night before, but it all seemed a blur.

Why had he been so insistent on coming up here, instead of going to the hospital the way Jill wanted? He didn't know. Somehow, last night, it had seemed important for him to get back to his own home.

Everything that had happened from the first moment of the attack now seemed distant and dreamlike. He couldn't remember any details clearly, just his trying to protect himself while blows rained down on his back and head, then sounds of shooting and a glimpse of a body on the pavement.

After that came disjointed fragments of memory. He remembered Jill waking him several times. She'd said something about people who'd been hit too hard on the head needing extra attention.

He reached up and gingerly felt the back of his skull. There were several lumps there. Then pain from his cracked rib hit so intensely he couldn't breathe for a minute. At last it passed, and he found himself gasping for air.

He splashed water on his face. Noticing the thick stubble on his chin, he found his razor among the discarded paint brushes piled along the back of the sink. He shaved somewhat sloppily. He kept nicking himself and realized how much he missed electric shavers. Since his back and head ached, he took a couple of pills to numb the pain.

Then he stumbled back to the bedroom, thinking of sleep. The strident buzz sounded again, making him turn in mid-step. He thought of the phone, the doorbell, the smoke alarm, but it didn't sound like any of those. He followed the sound into the living room.

He found Jill Washington sprawled out on his sectional sofa. The high pitched beep came again, from her waist. She rolled over at the sound and finally came awake.

"Damn thing," she muttered to herself. Then she noticed him standing there. "Well, good morning," she said. "So you're still alive, huh? And feeling like hell, I bet. You sure look it."

He nodded. "What's that noise?"

"It's my beeper going off. I ignored it the first time, but it looks like old A.J. Beaumont's getting impatient."

"You stayed here all night?" he asked.

"You were hit on the head. There could have been some brain damage. I had to make sure you didn't slip into a coma. If no symptoms show up during the day or two after someone's been hit on the head, then there probably hasn't been any damage."

"Yeah, I think I learned that, too, when I was ferrying troops in and out of riot zones for the Air Force. After one of those food riots there were a lot of head injuries."

"There sure were."

"You were on peacekeeping duty too, then?"

Jill nodded. "I was stationed in Europe mostly—London and Berlin. They'd gotten the food lines pretty much stabilized by the time I got my discharge. Bad times."

"Europe was tough," Cris agreed. "I was glad to spend the last few months of my tour training green pilots like you, something I actually enjoyed. I'd hate to be in the service now. Policing people at home would be worse than overseas. It looks like U.N. troops may end up here eventually, you know—they had riots yesterday in Chicago."

"Big ones?"

"Some of the worst yet. It's the drought. They've dropped harvest estimates for Florida and the south and had to cut rations by ten percent."

"No wonder," Jill said. "Many people can barely make do on the rations now. Although my parents own a farm, the drought's so terrible even they have to buy some rationed food. Some people use the black market, but they have only so much money."

"We've been lucky here in the northeast," Cris said. "Too much rain, if anything. A lot of people in the city grow their own vegetables now. I've got a garden on the roof myself."

"You're well off, then, compared to everyone else," Jill said. "One of my sisters spends a couple of hours each day in line to buy staples like bread, milk, and whatever fresh vegetables she can find. Her city water is rationed, too, and they don't have enough to spare for a garden."

"That's rough. Is she in the midwest?"

"St. Louis. The last I heard, they were having shortages of paper products. That should be hitting here soon."

"It already is," Cris said. "As if food rationing weren't bad enough."

"Even with the National Guard and local police running the food centers, I bet we have riots in New York before the year's out."

"I know, things have gone from bad to worse. That's why this stuff A.J. is talking about sounds so good. Marica seems to think his Pacifica project can feed millions."

"If he really lets it," she said, looking worried.

"What do you mean?"

Jill shifted her gaze away from his face. "As long as food is in short supply, it's worth a lot. Will he really solve the crisis . . . or just use it for his own profit?" She seemed uneasy. "Oh, never mind. I talk too much. I'd better answer Beaumont's beeper call or he'll be after me. May I use your phone?" She studied the glowing red phone number displayed on the beeper; that was the number Beaumont wanted her to call.

"Sure, it's over there by the telescope." He gestured toward the side of the living room where a six-foot-long tube seemed to be hanging on the wall. It was one of his favorite pieces, an exact holographic replica.

Jill glanced at it, then did a double-take. "Is it real?"

He laughed. "It fools most people. When you try to look through the viewscope, you see a hologram of the Andromeda Galaxy."

Jill picked up the phone from where it sat precariously balanced atop a pile of discarded canvases. "Sounds neat. Mind if I look more closely after my call?"

"Not at all. I'll find us some breakfast while you talk to Beaumont."

"Are you sure you feel up to it?" she asked, punching the number. "You don't look too well. As a matter of fact, I still think I should take you over to the hospital for a checkup."

Cris shook his head stubbornly. "I'm fine, really."

"Okay, okay. You're the boss."

Cris headed into the kitchen nook in the corner of his living room. As he fried up slices of tofu with some of his home-grown squash and tomatoes, he studied what was left of his weekly allotment of bread. It was almost gone. He glanced over to where Jill sat, half-sorry she'd been kind enough to keep watch on him through the night; that care would cost him a meal's rations.

Although his artwork provided him with an above-average income, extra food cost astronomical prices, even if he went to the black market. He never did. It didn't seem right for him to eat more than his fair share, even if he could afford it. But ration cuts were making it impossible to live, and it looked like his home garden soon wouldn't be enough of a supplement.

Americans, he reflected, had adapted well to rationing as long as it provided enough to eat, but inevitably they too would starve, like the rest of the world, and that meant more rioting, suicides, and even cannibalism. Take away a man's job and he'll find another; take away a man's home and he will live under the stars; but take away a man's food and he will fight.

"That smells good," said Jill interrupting his thoughts.

Cris added another dash of soy sauce to the stir fry. Then he took his last two slices of bread and toasted them. He didn't have butter for the toast, but a small bottle of homemade strawberry jam his mother had given him for Christmas would do just as well. He spread a half-teaspoon on each slice of bread slowly and evenly, as if each drop were priceless; and for all he knew, they were, for if the average temperature continued to rise and the droughts continued to spread as they had over the past twenty years, this could well be the last jam he would ever taste.

"Sorry there's no coffee," he said. "There hasn't been any in the stores around here for months."

"That's fine with me, I don't like it anyway. Water is my preferred drink anymore—far better the orange slop that replaced orange juice substitute, or that carbonated cola crap that tastes like walnut shells."

As Cris set plates onto the small, round table, Jill dug around in her purse. "Let me give you some meal coupons for this," she said. She handed him three green-inked papers similar to old-style dollar bills, but with a calorie count in the corners, 100, on each. He could use them in any public restaurant.

"No, that's all right," answered Cris automatically.

Sitting down, Jill waved him off. "Keep it. You probably can use it. Since I spend most of my time traveling, chauffeuring Beaumont around, I get travel chits—good for three full meals each and every day—probably twice as much food as the average person eating at home gets."

"Thanks," said Cris. "It will be nice to eat out for a change."

"You grew these veggies yourself?"

"On the roof. There are gardens popping up everywhere in Manhattan now—parks, window boxes, even some of the streets that no longer have any real function. The biggest problem is thieves. Since I have the top floor here, I'm the only one with rooftop access, so I don't have much trouble."

"What about the other tenants?"

He shrugged. "I gave a couple of them space up there too. Most people are too lazy to garden, though."

"I guess they think it's easier to steal, if last night's attack is any indication," said Jill.

"We haven't had too many robberies around here since the new self-defense laws went into effect. A lot of criminals got killed off in the early days."

"Unfortunately a lot of innocent people died too," added Jill.

Cris nodded. "I know—I felt there should have been some better way of dealing with drug problems. Better education maybe, or even legalizing some of the drugs so that they would be under a doctor's control. But it's easier just to let us all shoot one another . . ." An image flashed through his mind from the attack, the face of a young kid, who couldn't have been more than seventeen or eighteen, beating at him with a baseball bat. "They were just kids last night, weren't they?"

Jill sighed. "They still would have killed us. I have no doubt about that."

"Maybe they wanted money for more food. Is that possible?" He felt guilty, somehow, even though he'd been the victim.

"I don't know. I guess it's possible, since they cut rations again. People are scrounging to get by."

He remembered the body, how it had vanished so quickly. "I've heard rumors of extra meat on the black market lately," he said, almost to himself. "You don't suppose that's where the corpse went?" He felt pretty certain of the answer.

Jill nodded. "Cannibalism is happening all over the world—Europe, Asia, Africa. It could be here too. Some people are willing to pay any price for meat. A lot of people are eating their pets. And look at Beaumont—there's always meat on *his* table. Where do you suppose all the rich people like Beaumont are getting it?"

Cris shuddered. "Let's talk about something more pleasant, shall we, while eating?"

Jill said, "Like my assignment for the day? I'm supposed to go over to your apartment this morning, pick you up, and bring you over to the airport. Mr. Beaumont is going to fly you out to Pacifica so you can get a full view of the project." She paused to finish up her last bite of stir fry. Despite the fresh vegetables, the meal hardly seemed enough for the two of them. "Of course Beaumont had no idea I'd spent the night here. Perhaps it's best that we don't mention that fact. Actually, it really is quite nice that I did—very convenient for picking you up."

"So I'm supposed to drop everything and fly to God knows where for however long Beaumont wants?" Cris snorted. "He's got nerve, all right."

Jill looked uncertain. "You don't want to go?"

"Oh, I'm going all right. He's got me hooked, and he knows it." *And Pacifica is only one reason,* he reminded himself. "You couldn't keep me away now. And I won't tell Beaumont where you spent the night."

"Great."

"By the way, do you need a change of clothes, a toothbrush, anything?" he asked. He should have thought of that sooner. He wasn't much of a host under the best of circumstances, and last night he'd been so out of it, he'd hardly realized that Jill planned to sleep on his couch.

"No, that's okay. I always keep a spare toothbrush in my purse, just in case. Hacking heejees for Beaumont Industries, I only make it home about one night in three. The corporate vice presidents all treat pilots like personal servants—slaves might be a better word—at their beck and call any time of the day or night. Beaumont is just as bad, but he's signing the checks, so we all just take it. If you work for him, you will too."

"He doesn't sound like anyone I'd like to work for."

"If Beaumont wants you to work for him, you will. And he'll make that check so big you'll end up thanking him instead of cursing him when he makes you one of his lackeys. I know it all too well."

"I don't really need his money—I have plenty of commissions."

Jill laughed. "Cris, no matter how much money you have, it's never quite enough, is it? If money meant nothing to you, you wouldn't even be considering Beaumont's offer. Right? You'll work for him, it's all just a matter of price. You can bet Beaumont knows it, too."

"You're pretty smart. How did you ever end up working for Beaumont? After seeing you in action last night, and talking with you, I'm surprised you aren't running your own company."

"Don't I wish! You know, I did think of that once—that after I got out of the Air Force I'd start my own little rent-a-heejee spot out in Missouri, where my parents live. But the drought got worse and they were in danger of losing their small farm, so I took whatever jobs I could get." She looked troubled. "My family would probably be starving now, if I didn't have this job—not that it pays enough to do more than keep them alive—" She broke off abruptly.

Cris studied her face, really beginning to see her for the first time. She was very pretty, with creamy chocolate skin, a aquiline nose, and soft, sweet lips that seemed to always have a smile tugging at their corners. She seemed so young. But maybe that was just from his own viewpoint. Now that he'd crossed forty, a woman of twenty-five seemed almost a child.

He felt suddenly awkward and self-conscious. There hadn't been any women in his life since Marica, and for some reason he'd been thinking there never would be. *Marica's eyes, so blue you could lose yourself forever in their depths.* But now, as he looked into Jill's face, he found himself smiling broadly at her, with the smile of a man for a woman. And he began thinking of her as a woman, not just as a stranger or a heejee pilot or a possible new friend.

Jill shifted under Cris's suddenly intense gaze. She began stacking up the dirty plates.

"I'll wash the dishes."

"No you don't, guests don't wash up around here." Cris took the plates from her, gathered up their water glasses, and put them in the sink, already piled high with dishes. The dishwasher under the counter still worked, but he hadn't used it in a decade. *Damn rationing,* he mused. He turned on the hot water, tepid really, poured in a dollop of dish soap, and began to scrub a few dishes without much enthusiasm. When he finished almost enough to use for the next meal, he turned to find Jill admiring one of the holos in the living room, a sculpture of a little girl's head. He crossed to join her.

"How do you do it?" she asked.

"This one was easy. I took a plaster cast of Amber's head— that was the girl who posed—made a plastic bust, and set up lasers inside to project her image."

"It seems so lifelike, especially the way the eyes follow you when you walk around it," said Jill, circling the sculpture, clearly fascinated by its ability to shift and change as she looked at it from different angles. "It must have taken you months."

"A few days, really. It's nothing. Would you like to see a few others in my studio?"

"I think we can spare fifteen minutes."

A glimmer of jealousy made Cris ask, "Was Beaumont still at Marica's . . . the Vonn-Grendel estate?"

"I suppose so. The phone exchange was Long Island, not the yacht's international code."

"Damn him," said Cris.

"Is something wrong?" asked Jill.

"Sorry, no, nothing really." He took hold of her slender brown hand. "Let me show you the studio."

He led her over to the far side of the room, opened a pair of huge rolling doors, and pulled her into another large, open loft: his studio. Finished and half-finished holo-sculptures and holo-paintings dotted stands and easels around the room. Most were bright and multicolored, even garish and carnival-like. But the room as a whole looked more like an electronic junk heap than an artist's studio, with many computers and reels of fiber-optic filaments, lights, mirrors, lenses, lasers, switches, circuit boards, cameras, plastic pieces, and electronic parts all piled helter-skelter on the floor and workbenches.

Cris turned on the room's power supply and began to wander through the sculptures, turning on his favorites. Bits and pieces of Marica stared back him from every corner of the room. Dolphins with her eyes leaped dramatically from waves in a three-dimensional holo-sculpture suspended in mid-air from almost invisible wires. Wind carried her sigh through fields of golden wheat ripe for the harvesting.

Flowers the color of her hair spilled out of paintings and real vases. Birds, forests, children, and nature in her every form glowed and swirled and laughed and sang around them, captured forever in holographs.

Finally he brought Jill over to one of his newest sculptures, a rotating holo of a woman in a white sun dress sitting in a field of daisies. This was Marica made serene, a calmness and order given to her every move that the real Marica never had. *Beautiful,* he thought, *superb.*

As they approached the holo, the woman sat up straight, looked right at them, and tossed them a bouquet of flowers. Like most people who saw it, as she reached the critical distance, Jill reached out to catch the daisies. She gasped as her hands passed through them, then laughed as she realized she had been taken in by the apparent reality of the holo. In the holo-sculpture, eyes bluer than the sky blinked and almost seemed to wink at you. Then the full mouth parted into a wide smile that became a beguiling laugh, audible to the onlookers.

"I've used sound effects before, but I like this one the best."

Yet in his mind he heard another sound, the laugh transformed into a raucous, unpleasant gloating, like cawing birds . . . the laugh of a Marica who'd left him, who'd spurned his love for Beaumont's. In his mind's eye the sculpture twisted, showing the inner Marica instead of her lovely facade. A hag-like creature, part spider, part crow sat in a field of dung, throwing it toward him.

He shook his head, knowing that his hurt had produced the vision. Marica was neither the perfect fantasy woman of his holo, nor the horror his mind created. Something drove her to act as she did, to hurt him. He wished she had loved him enough to reveal the real Marica she tried so hard to hide. He would have liked to have painted that woman.

"This holo is wonderful," said Jill, bringing him back to reality.

"The miniaturized lasers, computers, and so on are all inside, and the illumination comes from here." He reached into the sculpture, where the daisies seemed to be. The illusion broke; he showed her the thick bed of fiber-optic cables underlying the holo. He prattled on, focusing on the technical details, burying his pain as he so often did.

"I'm working almost exclusively with internal projections these days. You can use pieces like this one anywhere, without any external lights. Micro power packs, like the ones in holo-clothing, can even make this totally portable."

"The woman is so beautiful, does she really exist?"

"No." No woman could ever be so beautiful or have the special combination of warmth and excitement he'd once thought he'd seen in Marica. "It's a fantasy, though it does look a little like my ex-wife."

"Ah, so you have been married then?" said Jill, glancing sideways at him. "I thought you probably were married, or had been, and not too long ago either."

"It's been about five months since the divorce. What made you think it wasn't too long ago?"

"Oh several things, but mostly the way you treated me. Any single man would have started asking me questions about myself hours ago, or maybe gone straight into a proposition. But you acted like a married man, or someone still thinking about his ex."

"I do think about her a lot . . . I guess that's why I keep painting her face."

"She left you, then? Or maybe you don't want to talk about it. I shouldn't pry. I'm always sticking my nose where it doesn't belong."

"She left me," Cris said slowly. "She's a remarkable woman in many ways, but for some reason she never had a great deal of self-esteem. It makes her feel better somehow to make conquests. Once we were married, I no longer interested her. She's after bigger game now, and it looks like she caught him."

Jill touched his hand sympathetically. "I'm sorry. For some people the grass is always greener elsewhere. Just keep telling yourself it's her loss."

"I do, but I can't help but miss Marica."

"Marica? Not Marica Vonn-Grendel?"

Cris nodded. Jill's hand seemed hot against his own. Glancing sideways at her, he was struck again by how pretty she was.

"Oh brother, I *am* sorry. I heard the people last night say that she and A.J. are engaged. Is he the big fish she caught?"

"Yes."

"Look, Cris, we shouldn't be talking about her, bringing up bad memories and all. Why don't you show me the rest of your studio and tell me all about how you make holos?"

The picture of Marica telling everyone about the engagement came unbidden to Cris's mind. It stung. He felt more depressed and tired. Suddenly he wanted to be away from the cluttered studio and all his memories of the past.

Making up his mind, he turned toward Jill and said, "That can wait for another visit. I think it's time for me to pack for the trip."

"Are you up to it?" she asked.

"Sure I am—I want to hear more about this Pacifica project."

"I really do want a grand tour of your studio sometime."

"It's a date. I'll have you back here soon." He laughed, and Jill smiled warmly.

As he took Jill's arm and escorted her back to his living quarters, he couldn't help but notice the softness of her skin, the way the light caught her eyes. He would paint Jill, he vowed then. As soon as they returned from Pacifica, he'd find an excuse to meet with her.

And his mind began to turn through the possible settings for her sculpture. A tropical forest, he finally decided, filled with red orchids . . .

SEVEN

"THERE'S PACIFICA," said Alexander J. Beaumont, pointing out the airplane's window. "That land on the horizon—see it?"

Marica tabbed off the boring fashion videotape she'd been watching, stretched languorously across A.J., and stared out the window. The ocean stretched beneath them like a giant blue-gray carpet, the foam dotting the top of the waves like bits of white fuzz. Beaumont's private jet had descended to a thousand or so feet above the water.

Marica felt utterly exhausted. They had been flying almost sixteen hours straight now, not counting the stopover for refueling in Los Angeles. Her ears ached from the constant roar of the jets and the change in altitude, her skin felt like sandpaper, and her hair hung in limp, dirty ringlets. She desperately wanted a bath.

Hopefully Rolugo Island wouldn't be too much of a disappointment. The pilot's announcements had made the weather outside sound ideal. With cloudless skies, warm South Pacific breezes, and gentle waves, Rolugo seemed a paradise. If only it offered a five-star hotel too, Marica thought, everything would have been perfect.

She didn't mind airplane travel unless the trips became too long. She never understood why so many people feared flying. The landscapes seen from a plane took on a dreamlike quality; you got a greater sensation of height from standing on a ladder.

Her father had always dreaded flying, perhaps more from the mere idea of it than true acrophobia. Whenever his bank had sent him on numerous business trips, he'd drunk himself into a stupor to overcome his fears. As he got older, the drinking became so commonplace that flying no longer made a difference.

The jet banked to the right and Rolugo vanished. Marica unbuckled her seatbelt and headed toward the plush couch on the other side of the passenger cabin.

Beaumont Industries' corporate plane had every luxury one could want aboard—bar, conference table, couches, computer console, and video links in the arm of every chair. It also had several obsequious stewardesses who catered to A.J.'s every whim with such eagerness that Marica found herself wondering how far they would go to please him. They annoyed her. Marica knew she shouldn't care, but somehow she did.

Stewardesses are sluts. She could remember hearing her mother say that before she even knew what those words meant. She knew it was a ridiculous stereotype, but she couldn't seem to push the memory away. She didn't know why she kept thinking about her parents today.

She glanced toward the pilot's compartment as she crossed the cabin, wishing she could see behind its closed door. Cris sat up there, next to that pretty black pilot, Jill Washington. That annoyed her, too.

Forcing her gaze from the pilot's cabin, she knelt on the couch and inspected the view from this side.

The kelp plantation floated on the ocean's surface like a giant greenish-brown flower. Fourteen mile-long `petals' radiated out from a central teardrop-shaped structure. Marica studied it carefully, comparing what she saw to the details A.J. bragged about during the flight.

Each `petal' consisted of a long line of linked mylar nets kept in place with plastic floats. Kelp rooted to the nets.

Large floats at the end of each 'petal' held round windmills, powering undersea pumps which pulled up nutrient-rich water to help feed the seaweed.

The central seeding station, resembling a deep sea oil rig, housed several dozen men and women who serviced the nets. They fixed tears and released any porpoises or whales which had ignored the sonic warnings of underwater transmitters and accidentally gotten caught. Their most important duty, though, involved rotating the nets.

Marica wondered what it would be like to live there in a simple life with the sea as one's closest companion. She remembered once, as a little girl, her parents had taken her to the ocean for a holiday. She'd been fascinated by the sounds—the constant dull roar of the ocean breaking on the shore, the gulls crying overhead, the crunch of sand beneath her feat. She remembered picking up some seaweed that had washed ashore. It hadn't smelled very good, yet somehow its novelty made it so interesting that she'd wanted to share it with her father. He'd batted it out of her hand hard enough to make her skin burn and yelled at her for picking it up.

A.J. had told her that seaweed grew quickly, at a rate of about two feet a day. His people would have been faced with massive harvesting problems if all the plants matured at once. Luckily Beaumont Industries' scientists had come up with an ingenious method to achieve continuous harvests.

The mylar nets slid down the mile-long line of floats. Each morning, workers at the center would seed and release new nets on each of the fourteen lines. Then the older nets would be moved farther and farther down the line. Close to the surface near the hub, the new plants grew quickly. As they aged, the nets gradually descended, from a few feet at the center to 200 feet at the far end, and the plants grew longer and longer, seeking the sun. By the time the kelp reached maturity at the 'petal's' end, three months would have passed.

Every day, ships circling the farm would harvest the most distant nets and reel the remaining ones outward. They'd detach the 200-foot-long kelp plants, chop them, press out excess water, and transport them to land for processing.

Each of the fourteen lines radiating from the central hub would eventually hold half a million square feet of net. Theoretically, such a system could feed almost half a million people each day.

But kelp wasn't the only product being farmed. The rich algae supported a thriving population of game fish. Trawlers plied the lanes between the fourteen 'petals', catching thousands of pounds of fish each day.

Her father would probably have thought such a system a total waste of effort. He hated seafood and had banned any sort from ever being served. Her mother went along with his edict, even though she was especially fond of shellfish. She never complained; over the years she'd learned not to.

Perhaps her father hated everything about the sea, thought Marica, including that seaweed. She hadn't realized it before, but Pacifica somehow appealed to her as a small way to get back at her father.

One of the stewardesses touched Marica's arm, breaking her concentration. "You're going to have to return to your seat," she said, smiling smugly. "We're about to land."

"Thanks," Marica said. Staring at the woman's short skirt and jaunty hat, she wondered whether her mother had been right about stewardesses. Certainly her father had affairs with enough of them.

She marched back to A.J., sat beside him, and buckled herself in place. Almost immediately the jet dipped and turned. Marica glimpsed another kelp farm on the horizon.

"How many farms are out there?" she asked.

"Two here are fully operational, and eight more are under construction," he said. "The island of Rolugo has the big processing plants. When we get the first two farms running to capacity next month, we'll see how close this pilot project meets our expectations. Eventually we'll build more in other locations." He smiled. "This project has exceeded our initial computer projections so far. For one thing, we didn't realize how much the fish would grow, feeding on the algae."

"What *are* you doing with all the fish?" she asked. "Aren't we too far away here to ship it anywhere?"

"Not with modern equipment. But we just ship out the best species. The less desirable ones are dried, ground, and mixed with the final kelp flour to give it more protein."

"Why didn't you put Pacifica in the Caribbean?" she asked with a hint of a pout. "It's closer to home."

A.J. shook his head. "Rolugo is a better base. It's just off the Samoan islands, but fairly isolated. We didn't want any other companies to get wind of we were doing until we had things everything working perfectly.

"We may expand into the Caribbean later, now that we've patented the whole system—the special netting, the processing, and most importantly, the bacteria used to break down the kelp's cellulose into starch."

"Won't storms rip the nets to pieces?"

A.J. smiled. "Our engineers have the whole thing worked out. The ocean's pretty quiet at the deeper depths. If there are storms, they'll just fill the floats with water and lower the nets. The central stations are flexibly anchored to the ocean floor. They can roll with waves without going anywhere."

The plane continued to descend; lush green vegetation appeared outside the windows. Marica leaned back and pressed her eyes closed. She hated landings. The plane's motion as it came in to land always made her slightly nauseous.

She wondered what her father would think when he heard about Pacifica. Wouldn't he be surprised to find out about her involvement? He'd be shocked to learn she'd married Beaumont and become one of the world's wealthiest women. She smiled—and he thought she'd never amount to anything.

She opened her eyes as the engines reversed thrust and brought them to a slow roll. Larger than she'd expected, the landing field included a modern-looking control tower and a gleaming new terminal building.

The plane didn't pull up to the terminal, though. It parked, and a gray-uniformed ground crew rolled a stairway over to the central hatch. The stewardesses had the hatch open by then.

As Cris and Jill Washington appeared from the cockpit, A.J. led the way down the stairs, into a hot, bright, humid, tropical afternoon. Marica squinted into the sun and followed.

"Goodbye," said one of the stewardesses.

"Have a nice day," said the other.

Sluts, thought Marica, passing them by wordlessly.

Exotic birds called from the jungle around the airport. Everything smelled fresh and earthy, so different from New York.

Marica didn't get much of a chance to look around. A.J. hustled her into a waiting heejee, and once again Cris joined Jill Washington in the pilot's compartment. Wondering how much pilots were like stewardesses, Marica felt an intense need to know just what they were doing up there.

She turned to A.J. "Don't you think Cris ought to sit back here with us? That way you can talk about Pacifica."

A.J. studied her a little too closely. "That's all right, we'll have plenty of time when we get to the villa. He seems to be getting along quite well with my pilot. I think I'll let her stay in the main house with us so she can keep him company."

Marica tried to hide her anger. "That's a good idea," she finally said, while she thought, *Like hell it is.*

"She seems like a nice girl."

"I'm glad you think so." He seemed amused.

Marica hid her sullen expression by snuggling up against A.J.'s side. She gazed out the window. Despite her best efforts to view Cris Morrisey as just one tool among many, she found herself inwardly stewing. He wasn't handsomer or kinder or richer than any of the other men who'd been in her life. It was something she couldn't analyze, it was just . . . *him*. She hated the way that Cris kept confusing her emotions. Maybe that was why she so often found herself teasing and tormenting him.

He loved her, she knew. *Really* loved her. That equalled power. Even when she hurt him, he kept coming back. Perhaps that was why she involved him in the Pacifica project—because she could see his hurt every time she kissed Beaumont. But she didn't love him, she told herself. She probably never had.

They flew over a stretch of jungle, then a small town that seemed to consist mostly of pre-fabricated houses. Following a road, passing over cleared fields gone to seed, they reached a sprawling, luxurious old-world style villa.

They landed by the front porch. Huge marble columns supported a red tiled roof; beyond them rose walls of native stone. Tall, narrow windows, all with black-painted shutters, looked down on the village and empty fields.

"It's . . . beautiful!" Marica said, looking at the vista that extended all the way to the blue Pacific.

A.J. smiled as he followed her. "This used to be a sugar plantation. My people gutted the villa and completely refurbished it. You won't find a single modern convenience missing."

Marica turned to see Cris helping Jill Washington from the pilot compartment. The woman held his hand like she enjoyed it. Biting her lip, Marica thought, *It isn't fair. She's going to ruin everything.*

"Is something wrong?" A.J. asked, sounding concerned.

She looked at him, lost for words. "My—my hairdresser," she finally lied. "Who's—who's going to do my *hair?*"

A.J. began to mutter platitudes about servants he'd brought in especially for her. Marica scarcely heard. She felt like a frustrated child whose toy had been taken away, and she knew it and loathed the weakness in herself.

Finally, mastering control of her emotions, she vowed to ignore Cris and his apparent interest in Jill. *He loves me. I can always get him back later.* Instead, she'd concentrate on A.J., Pacifica, and her upcoming wedding.

Allowing A.J. to believe he'd soothed her fears, she let him lead her inside. All the time her mind kept turning, spinning new plans within plans.

After a good night's sleep, Marica felt more like her old self. They had a leisurely breakfast in bed, watched latest food riots on the news-feeds from one of Beaumont's satellites, and began to adapt to the slow pace of South Pacific life.

By the time they rose and dressed, lunch was ready to be served in the dining room. Cris and Jill were already seated when they arrived. Marica stepped into the hostess role, and played it to perfection.

A.J. had also invited the head of the Pacifica project's operations, Michael Kramer and his girlfriend, Edie Dunn, an engineer at the geothermal plant.

"There's nothing like fresh fish for lunch," A.J. said as native servants wheeled in steaming trays. "I ordered mahi mahi as the main course, a local favorite. It'll melt in your mouths. The cook's a Samoan woman, but she's excellent. I had my doubts at first, but it turned out these Polynesians make good workers."

Marica thought of her father again. How he'd hate a meal like this. If he'd been here she could picture him knocking over the trays, slapping the servants, and screaming in a drunken rage.

Kramer nodded. "You know, the smartest thing I ever did was get involved in Pacifica. I hear everyone back in New York is trying to get transferred out here these days."

"It's our biggest project yet, no doubt about it," A.J. agreed.

"That's not why they want out here," Kramer said with a wicked grin. "It's never affected you, A.J., but in case you haven't noticed, there's a food shortage in the real world."

"But not on Rolugo Island," Cris said softly.

A.J. gave a little shrug. "We've tried to keep the project quiet, but there are always rumors. That's probably why so many of my top executives want in—not just their usual ambition, but unlimited food for their families. No rationing here!" He chuckled.

"It's certainly one perk I don't mind having," said Kramer. His shaggy gray eyebrows arched up, and he gave Marica a half-wink.

Old coot, thought Marica, instantly classifying him as someone she could easily control. His girlfriend, Edie, looked half his age, perhaps thirty, and quite pretty despite a drab, dark pantsuit and mousy ash brown hair pulled back into a severe bun. Edie might have been purposefully trying to look professional and unfeminine.

Marica, on the other hand, had chosen a scarlet sarong in keeping with Rolugo's Polynesian heritage. Jill wore a bright yellow and blue muumuu, and all the men except Cris wore loud patterned shirts that threatened to clash with one another. Cris wore a casual white shirt that somehow matched his noncommittal expression.

"When we first set up the kelp farms," A.J. said, "we didn't realize just how much fish we would get as a by-product. It's made this project more successful than I first hoped. The sea is tremendous resource that's been under utilized far too long."

Marica watched as A.J. wolfed down another plate full of the shrimp they had as an appetizer. She remembered the time her family had been invited out to eat at a friend's house and been served a seafood buffet. Her father had a fit. He'd started insulting the host and the man's wife, then had gotten into a fist-fight. She could still hear him drunkenly bellow: "Fish will kill you." Finally he'd packed his family back into their car and left, without letting them eat dinner. When they'd gotten home he'd beaten her mother half-senseless, saying that it all had been her fault—she should have told their friend not to serve fish. Marica had been sent to bed without her supper and had lain awake all night listening to her mother weeping in the next room.

As the servants brought out the main course of mahi mahi, Marica took a large serving and began eating it with gusto. She knew it was silly, but still she felt a secret thrill whenever she ate seafood.

"The sea is a source of power too," added Edie, between bites. "Did you know that the waves hitting a 60-mile coastline contain enough energy to power a million homes?"

Cris nodded. "I'd read that, yes. But the problem lies in tapping that energy. It's easier said than done—unless you've made some miraculous breakthrough?"

"Ironically, we've had the technology for some years," she answered. "One of Pacifica's goals is to make alternate forms of energy like ocean power economically feasible." She seemed to be warming up to the topic, like an experienced lecturer on home ground. "Petroleum, as we all know, is a limited resource. Its cost has increased so dramatically that power sources we once considered too expensive have now come within range."

Marica tried to look bored, letting her gaze wander out the picture window to the fields and town, and beyond them to the palm-tree lined beach. But she actually paid close attention to everything Edie said, thinking of how Pacifica could change the world for the better. The Beaumont name would become world-famous, and she'd be *Mrs.* Alexander Beaumont. No one could ever tell her what to do again.

Cris said, "A.J. mentioned his kelp farms could possibly supply power as well as food." He smiled coldly down the table at the industrialist, adding just loudly enough to be heard by everyone, "He'll *really* get rich then I guess."

As Cris deliberately baited Beaumont, Marica frowned. At first it had been fun to throw them together. But perhaps she had gone too far. By hurting Cris she'd sought to distance herself from him, but instead she found herself more drawn to him than ever.

Edie forced a smile and continued. "Well, kelp *is* a very fast-growing seaweed. It could be gathered and allowed to decompose in gas-tight vessels. You'd get about six cubic feet of methane for every hundred pounds of seaweed. But to produce any quantity of gas, you'd need thousands of miles of kelp farms."

"Besides," added A.J., "with the food situation as critical as it is, we can make more money using kelp as a food than as a power source."

"Actually," Edie said, "I'd rather use geothermal power. We're experimenting with that here, and some new solar cells as well. Part of the idea behind Pacifica—part of what makes us all so loyal to the project—is to make it a model for the world."

"Very commendable," Cris mumbled, looking at his plate. A.J. nodded, and Marica thought she glimpsed the shark behind the smile this time. A.J. loved showing the world what was good for it, she thought. His whole do-good campaign with Pacifica was really nothing more than a great big ego-trip. He'd love the acclaim he was going to receive for helping the environment . . . almost as much as he would love the profits from kelp.

"Pacifica may even help combat the Greenhouse Effect," said A. J. "We add iron to the water to encourage the algae's growth. The kelp absorbs carbon dioxide and releases oxygen."

He spoke confidently. "But there's more than that. We designed every inch of the project with the environment in mind, Cris. The costs may cut into Beaumont Industries' current profits, but in the long-run they will pay for themselves. Instead of getting dividends in currency, our stockholders will get the benefits of a cleaner environment. Eventually they'll receive more improvement in health and lifestyle at less cost than if they'd gotten cash dividends and used them to pay for those things. Saving the Earth is more important than profits."

Marica looked up in surprise. This didn't sound like the A.J. Beaumont she knew. Plowing profits back into environmental research and pollution-control hardly seemed his style. Cris and Jill also looked nonplussed, but Michael and Edie were nodding knowingly. In fact, Michael Kramer added a hearty, "That's right."

"You sound like you've joined up with the Green Age," said Cris skeptically.

A.J. laughed. "Those superstitious idiots—astrology, crystal power, reincarnation, and the like—what a bunch of crap."

"There's more to them than that," Marica countered. "Many of them are seriously seeking answers to life's questions. They're concerned about the environment and want to help reverse all the damage done to the planet. My friend Jade Moon is a member, and she's really quite sensible. She says God is nature, and we're all part of God, and so is the Earth. Destroying the Earth is like destroying God."

"You don't know what you're talking about," snapped Beaumont sharply.

Suddenly he sounded just like her father. Feeling as though she'd been kicked, Marica bowed her head and stared glumly at her empty plate. She felt like a child again, worthless and alone. The fish left a foul taste in her mouth.

"I worked for them, you know," added Cris. "I designed their logo. I don't think most of their leaders believe in God, or any of the Green Age's major tenets. They're too busy using their Church for their own ends. But I *will* give them credit, they *do* seem genuinely interested in the environment. It's kind of strange, when you think about it, to realize they're sincere about something."

"It's not all that strange," A.J. said, pushing his seat back from the table and standing. This signaled the others that the meal was finished, and they all began to rise.

Marica glanced around; no one seemed to notice her discomfort. She pulled herself together, smiled sweetly, and took A.J.'s arm as though nothing had happened. Her stomach knotted. She shouldn't have eaten so much fish, she thought; fish could kill you.

"No religion can become powerful unless its members have something real to believe in," A.J. continued. "The Green Age is as much a political organization as a religious one. It's always lobbying, getting candidates elected, urging members to boycott companies they don't find 'environmentally responsible.' But they won't give Beaumont Industries any more trouble once Pacifica goes public!"

"Is that why you're doing it," Cris asked pointedly, "to improve your public image?"

A.J.'s face reddened. "It's not just a publicity gimmick."

"Isn't it?"

"Kelp farming really will end the food shortage," said Michael Kramer, coming to A.J.'s defense. "And if Pacifica generates some good PR for the company too, what's wrong with that?"

"Then why haven't you already told the world about Pacifica, Beaumont?" Cris countered, an edge in his voice. "It might quiet some of the panic that's been going on lately—might stop some of these food riots."

"I'll be announcing it soon. The trick is not to excite everyone's hopes until we can actually deliver food. The first kelp beds have already been harvested, but we don't yet have enough of the processed kelp flour to begin distribution. I'll be making the announcement a couple of weeks after my wedding."

"I can't wait," Cris said sardonically.

Kramer nodded. "Things have been going very well here. All we need are more ships. We'll have all ten kelp farms fully operational by the end of the year."

"Well, are you all ready for the tour?" said Edie.

"Sure," said Cris, taking Jill Washington's arm. "Let's get out of here."

Marica grimaced slightly, then forced her most dazzling smile and squeezed Beaumont tightly. He stroked her hair as though she were a pet. She felt strangely unsettled and uncertain of herself.

"I won't be going with you," said A.J. "I know every inch of this place already, and I *do* have a company to run. Thank goodness for satellite communications! I'll leave you all in Edie's capable hands, and see you at dinner."

"Darling," Marica cooed, "you're so brilliant to have thought of this whole project. I'm lucky to have you." She felt a rush of emotion. She *was* lucky to have him. Suddenly insecure, she found herself wondering why anyone as important as he was would be interested in her.

As she flung her arms around A.J. and kissed him passionately, through half-closed eyes she watched Cris's face fall. Where once she would have felt only smug satisfaction, she now felt shame. Did she want to hurt him to stop him from loving her, or to stop herself from loving him? Shaken and uncertain, she tried vainly to push conflicting emotions out of her mind.

"This way," Edie said.

EIGHT

CRIS FELT a surge of anger as Marica rubbed against Beaumont like a cat in heat. He knew her enough to sense that this was a show as much for his benefit as A.J.'s, but that didn't make it hurt any less. He took a deep breath—and turned to Jill Washington.

"I can't wait to see the island," he said. His voice sounded almost normal. No matter how he tried, he thought, he couldn't seem to break his bonds with Marica. If only he didn't have to watch her fawning over Beaumont . . .

He cursed her for trapping him into this Pacifica deal. Not that he was committed to it yet. He told himself he was just looking the place over. He could leave any time he wanted. Then he smiled thinly to himself. At least his presence made Beaumont uncomfortable; he got the impression A.J. would just as soon be rid of him.

"I'm just glad Mr. Beaumont is letting me tag along," said Jill. "I've heard so many rumors about Pacifica."

Jill was pretty, intelligent, and congenial. They had a lot in common, Cris thought. Beaumont seemed to be trying to fix them up together. A.J. had suggested they both ride in the pilot's cabin on the airplane out to Pacifica, then they'd both flown up front in the heejee to the villa, and now they had adjoining rooms inside. And on top of everything else Jill would be accompanying their tour of Rolugo and Pacifica. *Interesting.*

"With Edie leading us," Cris said, "I'm sure it's going to be fascinating."

Jill smiled. "Technical, but interesting. She does seem to know her stuff."

"Right this way," called Michael Kramer from the doorway. Marica gave A.J. Beaumont a final caress, then joined Cris and Jill as they headed outside toward a long, pearl-white limousine.

Even on a tiny island in the South Pacific, Beaumont spared no expense for his comfort, thought Cris as he sank into the genuine leather seats. He found it impossible to believe that Pacifica was as philanthropic a project as Beaumont made it out to be. He was just too avaricious for that.

As soon as they'd climbed in, Edie accelerated. Cris didn't hear an engine.

"Electric?" he ventured.

"That's right." Edie grinned. "We've got a five hundred mile battery inside her. Takes four hours to charge." She pointed to a series of metal towers ahead of them. "That's the geothermal plant, our first stop. Those long buildings next to it are kelp processing plants."

*   *   *

The tour of the drilling towers proved interesting, if a bit dry. Edie Dunn spent twenty minutes explaining about the dangers and advantages of drilling in volcanic areas.

"It's possible to bore into rocks and steam reservoirs that are up to 350 degrees centigrade. In non-volcanic areas you can go down six or seven kilometers and only reach boiling temperatures."

Cris stared past her at the 100-foot metal framework supporting the drill. The geothermal plant powered not only Rolugo Island, but all of Pacifica. Underwater cables carried electricity out to the kelp farms.

Idly he let his gaze follow the electrical wires running to the main kelp processing plant. Sudden motion drew his attention. A man in ran along the roof of the building. *Strange,* he thought.

"Doesn't drilling also bring up poisonous gases?" asked Jill from beside him. She leaned back against the metal tower, taking advantage of its shade in the tropical sun. Edie had her full attention.

"That's true," said Edie. She stood facing them in the sunlight and was unaware of the man on the rooftop. "Sulfur dioxide is the big problem. We use pollution control equipment to eliminate the extra gases, but of course that's expensive. It's another of the reasons we're experimenting with the sun and the ocean as power sources . . . they're almost one hundred percent clean."

"Isn't there a way to tap the sun's energy by using temperature differences between the surface and deep water?" asked Cris, never taking his eyes off the man running along the roof.

"You're quite well informed," said Edie with some surprise.

"For an artist, you mean?"

"For anyone."

Thoughtfully, he pushed a lock of chestnut hair away from his face. "I've always been interested in nature, I guess. I've read plenty about our world and ways we might fix it, if anybody gave a damn about the Earth's future instead of creature comforts."

The man climbed down handholds and scampered along a six-foot-wide pipe to one of the kelp holding vessels, the size of a small petroleum storage tank. Inside bacteria caused fermentation. Cris wondered if something were wrong. The man should not have been using that route. There were plenty of access ladders and walkways to the holding-tank. The man reached the top of the tank and looked around. Cris thought of pointing him out to the others, but the man was probably just an ordinary workman.

"Well, the process you're thinking about is called Ocean Thermal Energy Conversion," Edie said. "But it won't work if the surface temperature is less than 40 degrees warmer than deep waters."

Cris nodded, without really listening, as he continued to watch the man on the roof.

The man had begun working at the access panel on top of the tank, apparently trying to open it. The others were either in the wrong position to see him, or too busy listening to Edie to notice him.

"You mentioned trying to tap the ocean's waves," Jill said.

Edie smiled. "That's something we've had more success with, using a variation on a scheme developed thirty years ago by a Scotsman named Salter."

Now that the man had gotten closer, Cris realized that his clothes looked wrong. It took him a moment to grasp the reason. The man was wearing a business suit.

Edie pointed down to the shoreline. "You can see part of it over there."

Cris shifted his gaze away from the strange figure long enough to see what she was talking about.

Floats of concrete, a hundred feet long and sixty feet across, lay in a line along the ocean's surface, attached together on a half-mile-long shaft. As waves struck, the floats tilted upward, revealing their duck shape, round on the front, with a tapered "tail end" pointing toward the sea. Leeward, the sea had become calm.

"They are called Salter's Ducks," explained Edie. "They absorb the wave's energy. The rocking starts pumps that circulate liquid inside a turbine, which drives a generator."

Cris turned back to the kelp tanks. The man seemed to be having trouble opening the access door—tugging, prying, pulling as he half-crouched. He yanked again, and suddenly it flew open. He staggered backwards and almost fell off the tank. An alarm began to wail somewhere inside the holding-tank.

Edie seemed oblivious to the sound, continuing her lecture. "We're studying several other methods of extracting wave energy."

Marica, Jill, and Michael Kramer had all turned to look at the man on the holding-tank's roof.

As the man knelt and swiftly reached inside the tank, one of the processing building's doors opened, and several uniformed men came running out. They looked like guards. At first they didn't see the man on the holding-tank, and they spread out among the holding vessels.

Not stopping to close the hatch, the man on the roof ran across the tank, climbed down, and sprinted toward the tanks nearest the geothermal drilling rigs. For a moment he vanished from Cris's view, but Cris could hear several short bursts of popping sounds—gunfire.

"What the devil is going on?" Edie turned to see what was happening, more drawn by her lack of audience than the sounds.

"Some fool up on one of the tanks," said Michael. "He must have tripped an alarm."

The man appeared again, running in their direction. He was a short, balding man, Cris now saw, whose toupee had begun to slide towards his left ear. He wore a lightweight gray suit, a blue shirt, and a dark blue tie.

"I know that man!" Michael exclaimed. "Bill Harrison, from the payroll office. What's he doing in the kelp tanks?"

The guards apparently weren't waiting to question Harrison. Two of them came racing after him, firing pistols at his back. The gunfire grew louder as they ran toward the drilling rigs.

Harrison darted left, dodging behind some large piles of unused pipes. More shots echoed, and one of the guards fell to the ground, clutching his side.

Cris and the rest of the tour group just stared in amazement. It didn't seem as if what was happening was real.

"What's in that tank that requires so much security? Isn't it just kelp?" Cris asked aloud, but no one seemed to be listening to him. "I think he took some, but what's the big deal?"

Harrison was still heading toward their position. Cris began to wonder if they should take cover, considering all the gunfire. Yet the danger seemed unreal; he felt frozen, as though observing a distant stage play.

"He must have been after the bacteria," said Edie. "That's truly the 'secret' part of the process. It is a new type, bio-engineered by Beaumont's labs. It transforms cellulose to starch. Without it, the kelp wouldn't be nearly as nutritious."

"Why wouldn't he take a sample after it's been processed, then?"

"We microwave the kelp during drying," Michael said. "That kills off any living bacteria so that it can't be replicated. The kelp itself doesn't matter—it breeds through spores, so this strain is bound to spread around the world. The bacteria makes commercial processing economical."

"Aren't any of you paying any attention?" said Jill angrily. "There's a man running for his life over there, and you're lecturing us on kelp farming!"

"Sorry, I just—"

Edie's answer was cut short as several shots rang out around them. She collapsed in a heap, blood streaming from a small hole in her chest.

"Get down!" Cris shouted, his Air Force training finally taking over. He hit the ground and rolled next to a bush. Marica and Jill darted into the tower, taking cover behind its steel beams. Michael dashed for the limo and crouched down behind the polished trunk.

Harrison had emerged from the pile of pipes, seen them, and started shooting at them as he ran toward their car. Only one guard now followed him, and he too was shooting in their direction.

Harrison whirled suddenly, firing at the guard. The lower half of the man's face blew apart, and he dropped. For an accountant, Harrison seemed to be an unusually fine shot, thought Cris.

Clearly Harrison headed for their car, so Michael Kramer bolted for the tower. Harrison saw him and deliberately shot him in the back of the head. Kramer's white hair became scarlet as he stumbled forward, then fell motionless, near Edie Dunn.

Cris gasped as reality seemed to snap back into place. He was no longer a dispassionate observer. He was lying within twenty feet of the electric limousine, a low palm bush his only concealment, with a deadly madman coming toward him.

And he wasn't worried only about himself. Harrison might spot the two women hiding in the rig and go after them. Cris had no gun, no weapon of any sort, and didn't know what to do.

For a split second panic set in. He thought of burrowing into the sandy ground, of playing dead and praying that Harrison would pass him.

The accountant had almost reached the car and was bound to spot him any second.

There's no time to panic, a crazy thought whispered through his head as he reached into his pocket to see if he had anything he could use against Harrison. There was only his small sketchbook and a pencil.

He took out the sketchbook, gritted his teeth, and flung it as hard as he could behind Harrison.

Harrison halted and half turned at the sound of fluttering pages. The sketchbook slid across the sandy ground. At that moment, Cris jumped up and dived at the man.

He heard the blast of the gun and felt its heat sear his face as Harrison whirled back toward him. Then his tackle connected, and he was on top of the smaller man, pounding him with his fists. Anger and adrenaline surged through him. Cris was hardly aware of the blood on his hands. Harrison had become a monster instead of a man, some *thing* to be stopped. He hit him over and over.

"Stop it, stop it, Cris!"

Hands seized his shoulders, pulled him back.

"Cris! *Stop!*"

Marica's voice pulled him back from the brink of the madness that had claimed him once before.

"Oh god," he said, dropping his hold on Harrison. The man slumped to the ground, his face a bloody pulp, one side of his ribs half caved-in from the force of the blows. Cris stared at his blood-covered hands, unable to believe what he'd done.

It had been like this once before, during the European food riots. He'd been ferrying troops to control the crowds at food distribution centers in France. When the supplies ran out, pandemonium broke loose. A group of men had surged forward and started taking the food away from some women and children who had already received it. Fighting escalated as the airmen tried to disperse the mob.

Cris had seen a Frenchman bash in a woman's head for her loaf of bread. It had set him off. By the time he'd finished, he had literally torn the man apart with his bare hands.

Cris shuddered at the memory. That had been the day he'd decided to leave the Air Force. The counsellors had talked him into training duty in the States instead, and he'd stuck it out for a few months. But he'd never forgotten what he'd done, and he'd vowed never to draw blood again.

Slowly he backed away from Harrison. The murderous rage that had washed through him like a summer storm had vanished as quickly as it came.

Jill now held Harrison's gun. She emptied the clip and slipped it into her purse.

Two security guards appeared. Marica hurried over to them, explaining what had happened.

Jill had been taking care of the wounded. Bending over Harrison, she pulled open his shirt and examined him.

"Did . . . did I kill him?" asked Cris.

"The bastard's still breathing," she said. "I can't say the same for Michael Kramer though."

"What about Edie?"

"She ought to make it."

Marica ran back to Cris.

"That blood, it's not yours is it?" she asked.

Cris looked down. Crimson streaked his shirt, and his hands were dripping wet.

"I don't think so—the bullet missed me."

"You've got a burn mark on your face. Oh, Cris, I was so afraid I was going to lose you!"

Marica pressed against him. Love and concern filled her warm blue eyes.

He wanted to hold her forever, to take comfort from the strength of her arms, to find forgiveness in the touch of her hands. But in his mind's eye he pictured her draped over Beaumont, with A.J. leering up at him. Beaumont's face seemed a mask behind which lurked something cold and calculating. All the time Marica seemed to smirk at him with a smile that tormented and teased.

He pushed her away brusquely. "I'm all right. I'll be just fine."

"I think this is what he stole," said one of the guards. He held up a small flask. Inside was a thick greenish-brown mass of bacteria-laden kelp.

The bottle's label had just one neatly lettered word: *Pacifica*.

NINE

JILL TRIED to look calm as she checked Harrison's pulse. She felt dazed and confused. The realization that Harrison had probably been a paid agent, perhaps even in Jade Moon's employ, amplified the horror of what had happened.

It hadn't really occurred to her that spying on Beaumont could be a dangerous. What if they caught her stealing papers? She'd assumed at the worst she'd be fired — but what if that turned into being fired on, by guards?

Of course Harrison had obviously been no casual spy; he'd tried to kill anyone in his escape path. He'd probably been the agent of a foreign government or a rival company.

Unnerved, she suddenly resolved to see Jade Moon and return her money, no matter how much her family needed it.

"We'll take over now, Miss," said one of the guards.

She stood and nodded. The faint wail of the alarm was joined by louder sirens. In a few moments two ambulances and several patrol cars arrived.

Pulling herself together, she went to Cris. Dark smears of blood marred the limousine's pristine white exterior where he leaned against it. He looked shattered.

"Oh God, Jill, I couldn't control myself—I just kept hitting him."

"It's all right." She reached out, and he came to her, clinging to her for support like a lost child. "You had to stop him." She knew from her own experience how he felt. When something like this happened you reacted out of instinct, and sometimes you lost control of the violence inside. "It's not your fault."

Stroking his long hair and hugging him, thinking of Jade Moon and Harrison, she hardly noticed the arrival of several more company heejees. More guards, medical crews for the wounded—and A.J. Beaumont.

"God damn it!" Beaumont roared like a bull elephant.

Jill jerked upright.

Rage contorted A.J.'s all-American good looks into a frightening caricature. "Where is he?" he shouted. Spotting Harrison, Beaumont charged forward, pulled the injured man up off the ground, and began violently shaking him. "Who are you working for?" he demanded.

The guards tried to calm him, to coax him away from Harrison, but that only made him more furious.

A.J. twisted one of the accountant's arms until it reached an obviously abnormal angle. Harrison's eyes remained closed, and his mouth remained silent. He didn't even whimper. He probably couldn't have spoken even if he wanted to, since Cris had already broken his jaw. Besides, Jill realized, the accountant may not have regained consciousness after that beating.

Beaumont hurled the man down in disgust and began kicking him.

"Stop it," cried Cris in distress. "Can't you see what I've already done to him?"

Before Jill could stop him, Cris ran to Beaumont and tried to pull him back.

"You stupid ape!" Beaumont swung around abruptly and began pummeling Cristopher.

Marica screamed, "A.J.—no!"

Beaumont's ever-present bodyguards rushed forward, ready to protect their boss.

But Cris just covered his head and ducked back. It had to be taking every bit of his will power, Jill knew, but he didn't hit Beaumont; he didn't defend himself in any way. That seemed to make Beaumont angrier. One of his jabs hit Cris's nose, and it began to bleed.

The two bodyguards just watched. Their boss had instigated the fight, and unless he seemed in danger, they would not intervene.

With Beaumont's vicious disposition, Jill knew that annoying him could cost her job. But she had to do something.

She inserted herself between the men, yelling, "Please, Mr. Beaumont, Cris just saved our lives!"

Marica had moved at the same moment. The slim woman grabbed Beaumont's shoulders, holding him back.

"A.J., you must stop. Darling, please . . ."

"All right, all right!" Pounding his right fist into his left palm, A.J. finally stepped away from Cris. "God damn it, Marica—Harrison tried to steal my bacteria, and God knows what else, and then this stupid ex of yours gets in my way. I want to give Harrison what he has coming to him."

"There is no use of that now, sir." A medic called from Harrison's side. "The man is dead."

"Damn it!" cried Beaumont.

"We've found something on him, sir," said one of the island guards meekly, afraid of arousing his boss's wrath. He held up a pendant that was still chained around the dead man's neck.

As the sun hit it, Jill could see a holograph of a bluish-green Earth. With a sinking feeling she recognized it—the Green Age logo, worn by many members of the Church. Suddenly she felt guiltier than ever for taking the Green Age's bribe.

"So those people are behind it," said A.J. thoughtfully. He seemed to have regained his composure. "Damn environmentalists. Just for once I thought I'd finally beaten them to the draw with Pacifica, but they're never satisfied no matter what I do."

"He must have been a GAN," Jill said, remembering the Green Action Now! terrorist tendencies. The GANs were the radical splinter group of the Church of the Green Age which had given Beaumont the most trouble over the years.

"Of course he was," said Beaumont, "or worse." He waved his hand toward Michael's body and to the stretcher where Edie lay. "Who else would kill with such brutality?"

One of the medics went to work on Cris, cleaning his bloody nose, wiping the blood off his hands with a towelette.

"I don't understand," said Marica. "All Green Agers, even the radicals, want to protect the environment. Why would they try to hurt the Pacifica project?"

"That's right," added Cristopher. "The Green Age should support you if Pacifica is all you say it is, Beaumont."

A.J. glanced at him sharply. Then he shrugged and said, "Who knows. Harrison was probably just plain nuts!"

Stepping close to Cris, he said calmly but firmly, "I've had just about enough of you, Morrisey. I want you off this island."

"Does that mean I'm you don't want me working on the Pacifica project?" asked Cris disdainfully.

"You bet it does."

Marica pressed against A.J. "But darling, you know how useful it would be to have someone as well known as Cris involved."

Beaumont appeared immune to her charms this time. "I don't care how good an artist he is, or how famous. I'm sick of having him around, following you like a dog and snapping at me." He glared at Cris. "Get cleaned up and then get out of here, Morrisey."

Cris smiled wryly. "Delighted. It's clear that working for you would be about as pleasant as rabies."

A.J. turned to Jill and for a split second she feared he would target her for his wrath as well. But all he said was, "Washington, fly him out of here ASAP. Then return and pick us up." He turned abruptly away, dismissing her without another thought.

"Yes, sir." She felt as though she were in the Air Force again, kowtowing to the high brass. Beaumont had treated her like a guest only as long as it had served his purposes. Marica's ex-husband obviously made him jealous. He'd encouraged Jill's friendship with Cris to keep him away from Marica. Exiling Cris from Pacifica signaled her return to the status quo—a paid chauffeur at his beck and call.

Cris seemed almost in shock. Jill half-pushed, half-dragged him into one of the company heejees, and they headed back toward the villa with several guards.

The more Jill thought about it, the more her resentment grew. She'd known all along she couldn't really expect more from A.J., but his brusqueness still grated.

It would serve him right if someone stole his plans, she thought. But remembering what had happened to Michael Kramer, Edie, and several guards, she knew the price had been too high.

Had Harrison really been a GAN? They used terrorism to stop any project they felt would hurt the environment. She thought she'd read that they'd disbanded long ago, but perhaps they'd hidden within the Green Age. She wanted no part of them. *If Jade Moon were behind it . . .*

She still had the money she'd accepted from Jade. Luckily things had moved so fast she hadn't had time to send it to her parents. She'd return it to Jade Moon at the first opportunity, she was certain of that now.

For the first time in days, she felt the weight of her conscience begin to ease.

The trip back to New York proved routine, if time consuming, and for once Jill was glad.

When they finally reached the city, she requisitioned a company heejee and took Cris home. City Control brought them quickly to Cris's block. Now early afternoon, the block looked almost deserted and seemed fairly safe. However, she watched the monitors with greater than usual care as they landed.

"I'll give you a call soon," he promised with a light-hearted grin he probably didn't feel. "We still have to finish your tour of my studio, don't forget."

"I'd like that," she said. She felt awkward and tongue-tied. Finally she squeezed his arm. "Take care of yourself, Cris. I'm sorry about Beaumont and Pacifica, but . . ."

"I understand."

She nodded, and he climbed out. She watched closely as he safely entered his apartment building.

She doubted she'd ever hear from Cris again. Even though he seemed to like her as much as she liked him, clearly he still loved Marica. How could they ever be more than friends? It had been a couple of years since Jill had been seriously involved with a man, and she wouldn't fall into a relationship casually.

Would she want a relationship with him, anyway? Cris Morrisey seemed a very different type of person than she was, and he was older by at least a decade . . . Still, she found herself attracted to him. He was intelligent, warm, and sensitive, with an appealing face and personality. She could imagine how something more than friendship might develop.

But her major priority had to be keeping her job at Beaumont Industries, she decided, and keeping herself out of the sort of trouble Harrison had gotten into.

Using the radio, she tied into the city phone system and called Jade Moon to set up a meeting. Jill figured she had just enough time to see Jade, then grab a couple hours of sleep, before returning to Pacifica to pick up Beaumont and his fiancee. To her surprise, Jade told her to come over at once. She agreed.

The New York headquarters of the Church of the Green Age had once been known as the RCA Building at Rockefeller Center. A Japanese company had owned it before climate changes caused almost continual typhoon winds to sweep across their islands, bringing destruction, starvation, and economic ruin.

The building looked much as it had twenty-five years before, except for a two-story glass pyramid added onto the roof. Tourists still paused to gaze down on the basement-level lower plaza, but they no longer watched twirling ice skaters. Power shortages had made the rink too expensive even before the Green Age bought the building.

Instead, tourists stared with curiosity at several primitive huts made of willow branches. The Green Agers called them "Earth Houses," modeled on Native American ritual cleansing "sweat lodges." The Green Agers had incorporated the idea into their religion from the Light Worker New Age movement in the '90s. Here, privileged Green Agers meditated and became spiritually cleansed.

The bronze Prometheus statue, covered in gold leaf, remained in the plaza, looking much the same as it had years before. However, now layers of dried flower garlands left over from the last Earth Meditation Day event hung from its shoulders like a cape.

Jill ignored the onlookers and headed for the fence at the top of the stairs. She gave her name to one of the guards at the sentry box. After checking her ID, he unlocked the gate.

"Jade Moon will meet you in House One," he said, pointing at the smallest sweat lodge.

Jill had been here once before, when Jade first contacted her. She never did figure out why Jade thought that she might be willing to spy on A.J. From the things Jade said, Jill gathered that some Green Agers were already Beaumont Industry employees. Perhaps they'd seen her employment records and thought she would be corruptible.

She felt uneasy realizing how much the Green Agers knew about her, and even more uncomfortable that they'd been right. She did have a price.

As she passed the largest lodge she could hear voices inside chanting, "I am God, I am God, I am God." Then the sweet voice of a young boy sang out, "I am the light and there is no darkness; I am the love and there is no fear; I am the Earth and there is no famine; I am the beginning and there is no end."

The lodges were round, vaguely turtle-shaped. She reached

House One and entered through a tunnel made of willow branches that formed the turtle's neck. The low ceiling made her stoop. Inside the turtle's belly it was very warm and very dim. Jill stood straighter. Modern heaters had replaced the heated rocks that the Native Americans would have used to produce the sauna-like effect. Glass blocks containing soft lights sat in the corners, casting odd shadows on the willow-branch walls. Hardened earth covered the floor.

A half-dozen roughly-hewn wood benches faced the small alcove in the front that represented the turtle's head. Several sacred objects to be purified lay on the knee-high granite altar—feathers, seashells, a crystal goblet filled with grain, and several large quartz crystals. The Green Agers believed crystals could be used to channel in good energy and clear away bad.

Jade Moon knelt before the altar, whispering a chant: "I am God, I am God, I am God," over and over like a Hindu mantra.

Jill stood silently, not wanting to interrupt. She felt awkward and out of place. She'd given her word to Jade, and now she planned to take it back. *Was that any worse than agreeing to spy on A.J. in the first place?* an inner voice taunted.

Suddenly Jade seemed to sense her presence and broke off her prayer. "Ah, there you are. Have you brought some papers? I heard you went to Pacifica. Were you able to collect any interesting information?"

If Jade Moon's informants knew her movements, Jill wondered why they weren't able to steal enough information themselves. Perhaps they weren't in as close contact to Beaumont as she was. *Perhaps they had tried and failed,* she thought, remembering Harrison.

"No," she said. "I haven't brought you anything." Then, on a sudden hunch, she added, "And don't expect Harrison to bring you anything either—he's dead."

Jade Moon didn't show any emotion, but her brown eyes shifted just enough at the name to convince Jill: Jade had known the accountant.

"Harrison?" Jade said slowly. "Who is Harrison?"

"Your agent on Rolugo. They caught him stealing the bacteria and shot him."

"I've never heard of him."

"Of course not," Jill said sarcastically. She pulled off her belt, opened its hidden compartment, and removed the money. Holding it out, she felt a wave of relief. "I've decided not to take your offer."

Jade shook her head. "We'd hoped to have your voluntary cooperation. However, you no longer have any choice—you *will* help us . . . one way or another."

She reached behind the altar and flicked a hidden control. The red lights of lasers suddenly blinked over the benches, projecting a three-dimensional holographic movie.

Jill saw herself standing on Marica Vonn-Grendel's rooftop among the silent mannequins. Their goofy grins seemed more mocking than friendly now. In the stifling heat of the room her skin became as cold and clammy as the arctic night.

"One hundred thousand dollars, plus we'll give you a regular monthly salary," Jade's voice came from the holo.

She saw herself take the envelope.

"You are going to be helping the whole world."

She saw herself stick the envelope into her belt pouch. The holo blinked off.

Even in the gloom of the sweat lodge, Jade Moon's white teeth seemed to gleam as she smiled. "We have the whole thing on holodisc, as well as a copy of the very first conversation you and I had in this place. Spying on your employer is illegal, Miss Washington. And, of course, there's no telling what someone as powerful and immoral as Alexander James Beaumont might do if he found out he's been crossed."

"I see," Jill managed to whisper. Sweat beaded on her face. The air felt thick, stifling.

"Why don't you keep that money, Miss Washington? Your family needs it. The faithful have gladly given it to us, and we pass it on to you to help the cause. Whether you take the money or not, you *are* going to do as you are ordered."

Jill felt the net close and tighten around her. "I can tell Beaumont about you."

Jade Moon nodded somberly. "Go ahead—you'll still end up in jail. Then explain to your family why you've lost your job, and why they'll starve on the streets."

The pounding of Jill's heart seemed like a jackhammer. She had failed her parents and her family.

Jade went on, "We need a sample of that bacteria, or a copy of its technical specifications. You will get them for us."

"Why? Beaumont is planning on making the announcement about Pacifica in a few weeks. When he does, all this will become public knowledge."

Jade lifted the largest crystal from the altar and rubbed her fingers over its pointed top as though it were a talisman. "Don't you understand? Beaumont will keep the process a secret. That's the only way he can control it. He's going to lessen the food shortage, all right, but he won't end it. He'll keep his prices and profits up. I know what I'm talking about. I know the man well; he and I used to be quite close before I realized what a bastard he really was."

"If Harrison couldn't get the bacteria, and he lived on Rolugo, how do you expect me to?" asked Jill, no longer certain she believed Jade's explanations. "I couldn't get past security and into the plant." Then a terrifying thought hit her. *If Harrison were a GAN terrorist, Jade probably was one too.*

"Perhaps not," Jade said. "But you might get access to Beaumont's briefcase when you ferry him around. He can't keep his eyes on it all the time. You might be able to get some information from that. We've already gotten a few of the specifications we need, but not everything . . . yet."

Harrison must have passed on a lot of information, thought Jill. He'd been in a good position to learn about Pacifica's non-polluting energy sources, as well as the kelp farms.

"Just do the best you can," Jade continued. "If we don't get the data on the bacteria soon, we may have to try something more drastic. If that happens, you'll do what I tell you to do, and you won't question it. Do you understand?"

How far would I go to protect myself? Jill wondered. *How far would I go to protect my family?* The heat made her dizzy; she felt a trickle of sweat down her back.

"I'm not going to kill anyone for you," she said.

Jade Moon's eyes narrowed, appraising her. "Let's hope it doesn't come to that."

TEN

CRIS HELD the pencil sketch he'd just finished at arm's length, turning it critically. It showed a cross-section of the ocean. On the bottom half, under the water line, a large kelp plant dominated. Roots anchored it to a net in several places. Reef-dwelling parrotfish, tangs, and butterfly fish darted through the kelp's fronds, nibbling a bit here and there. Larger edible fish such as bluefin tuna, snappers, and square-headed mahi mahi circled peacefully behind. Above the water you could see a pelican perched on a float. The net linked to a distant central hub, a complex mini-city straight out of some science fiction magazine.

This sketch could be the basis for his next bit of holo-art — part sculpture, part painting, part photograph. When he closed his eyes, he imagined it complete, the audio track of whispering waves, the faint cries of pelicans . . .

The image soothed, reassured. It glistened with hope and promise. It would have been perfect to kick off Pacifica's publicity campaign. *Food for millions! The wonder of our generation! Pacifica!*

Cris snorted at the thought. It was all so much hype and wishful thinking. He had better things to do with his time. Shifting his sketch again, he studied it in shadow. The strands of netting took on a darker hue. The fish looked subtly skeletal, the pelicans almost predatory.

He closed his eyes and imagined. Kelp nets cast shadows through the water; barracudas circled the kelp, teeth bared. There would be vultures overhead. *Pacifica—helping to pick your bones clean.*

He liked it. It had a certain vicious charm. Perhaps he'd do it that way and put it in his next show.

Then he thought better of it, sighed, and crumpled the sketch in his fist. He didn't want to think about Pacifica. He didn't want to think about Marica or Beaumont or anything else except his work. He just wanted to draw tonight.

Flopping down on his studio's couch, he pulled the over-sized sketch pad onto his lap. It was time for a change, he told himself. How long since he'd used charcoal? Months, at least. He found a charcoal stick on the floor near the wall, drew a hesitant line on the pad, curved it into a cheek. When he added a curl of hair and a few lines hinting at eyes and lips, the image burst out.

Marica. Of course it was Marica.

He went on drawing, faster now, like an sculptor chipping away marble to reveal a statue. Marica, standing on the water like Jesus, arms outspread while all the fish and birds came to her, so beautiful . . .

He ached inside. Damn her, why couldn't she leave him alone? His face felt hot and his eyes burned. No, he wasn't going to cry over her. He wasn't even going to think about her.

He hurled the pad away from him and watched its pages flutter like a wounded bird until it crashed against the far wall.

He should be painting the stark beauty of metal drilling rigs boring into the Earth, he told himself. He should be capturing the essence of electricity in waves and sunlight. There couldn't be any human figures. On Rolugo, he'd believed in the sea's power. Like a magic charm, it could save the world from destruction. It should be sparking his imagination. Why wasn't it?

Instead, when he closed his eyes, he saw Marica. She stood next to Beaumont, her arms around him—*kissing* him.

Something buzzed, and he jumped half a foot, startled. Then he realized it was his door. It felt like years since he'd had visitors.

He crossed to the intercom and punched the button. The video cameras in his building's entrance had been smashed months ago; all he got now was the voice, which crackled and hissed into something almost indecipherable.

"Yes?" he asked.

"It's Jill," a woman said.

It took him a moment to realize who it was. Jill Washington. Of course.

"Jill—hold on I'll let you up."

He pushed the button to open the building's front door, then waited impatiently for her to arrive. At last the elevator opened, and she entered.

He almost didn't recognize her. With her shoulders slumped, dressed in wrinkled and dirty clothes, she didn't look like the same person. Sweat gave her face a waxen sheen. She looked like she'd been through an all-night workout.

He hadn't seen her since she'd dropped him off three days before. He'd assumed she'd flown back to Rolugo Island and resumed her duties—but now he wondered. Something bad had certainly happened to her.

"I'm sorry I didn't phone," Jill said in a weary voice. "I just had an impulse to see you. I hoped you'd be here." She tugged nervously at the single long braid of hair against the side of her face like a black rope. "You don't mind, do you?"

"Of course not," Cris said. "You look like hell."

Jill looked away from him in embarrassment. "I haven't had much time for sleep, with this flying back and forth to Rolugo, even if I could sleep . . ."

"What happened?"

"What do you mean?"

"On the island. Was there more trouble? Is Marica okay?"

"Oh, your ex-wife. She's fine. She and Beaumont are getting ready for their wedding. It's on his yacht this Saturday."

Cris turned and hit the wall with his fist. The pain helped. He felt all cut up inside, suddenly, and didn't know what to do.

Jill edged back nervously. "Maybe I shouldn't have come. This is probably a bad time."

Cris forced a smile. It dropped neatly into place like a mask. "Oh no, it's fine." Slowly he massaged his throbbing hand. "I can use a break. Nothing I draw seems to be going right anyway."

"You're sure?"

"Sure." He shrugged. "Come in, make yourself at home. Is there anything I can get you?" He closed the door, then went to the couch and cleared room for her. Pictures seemed to drift around his apartment like a canvas and pasteboard tide when he didn't keep on top of them.

Jill perched on the end of his couch slowly, as though still uncertain. She said, "I'm feeling old and tired, Cris. Beaumont orders me around like a slave. He pays overtime, but after awhile the exhaustion starts to mount up. And when that guy Harrison showed up and the killing began, it just really got to me."

"How is Edie Dunn doing?"

"She'll be out of the hospital in a few days. If you're wondering about Harrison, I haven't heard anything more about him—it's as though they're all hushing it up. Beaumont tightened security on Rolugo, though. It's like a prison camp now."

Cris nodded again, more slowly this time, not saying anything. He studied Jill, but her eyes shifted around the room, looking everywhere but at him. She wasn't telling him everything, he decided.

"You've been busy working?" she asked.

"Trying. I keep thinking about the ocean and Pacifica and that leads me back to a dead end. I shouldn't have gone out there."

"It's Marica, isn't it?" Jill said. "You still love her."

It was more statement than question, Cris decided. He didn't know how to answer. He stared at the far wall, at a few of his older works, done when he'd just worked in oils.

At last he said, "I'm not sure what I feel any more." *Her smile, like sun on water . . .* He shuddered and tried to force her from his thoughts. "I could give you that tour of my studio now," he suggested.

"Sounds like fun."

He stood and felt strangely awkward. Looking around, he realized he didn't know where to begin.

"Why don't you tell me more about holography?" Jill said.

"Ah, good idea." He led her toward the far corner of the room. Here he had some of his larger displays set up, experimental models of several of his more famous works. He found the control panel, searched the settings, powered the displays.

"Mirrors bend coherent light—light of a single color from a single source such as a laser—so that it curves into shapes which human eyes can perceive as objects. It's trickery, illusions played out on the optic nerve. Any eye or lens that catches light refracted the right way will perceive a picture."

"But you can look at it from any angle."

"If the eye moves it will see a different wave and a slightly different object. That makes the illusion three dimensional. Of course, with the miniaturization of lasers and all the other advances in holography, as well as the use of nano-technology, there have been a lot of changes from the primitive holograms that used to exist. We've got holo-fabrics now that use nano-technology and new fiber optic materials. We can even arrange holographic projections around solid objects, totally transforming them into something else to the naked eye, though it becomes more difficult if the interior object moves."

He pointed to a large open plastic box about the size of an old-fashioned typewriter. It contained a computer, circuit boards, miniature lasers, and wires that trailed outside into a test panel. "Take a look at this, I'm working on it as a present for Marica and Beaumont's wedding."

He flipped a switch and suddenly the three-dimensional figure of Alexander James Beaumont appeared where the box had been. He wore a dark grey business suit. Life-size and lifelike, it appeared indistinguishable from the real thing. The figure smiled directly at Jill.

"It's incredible," she whispered, somewhat shaken.

"I computerized his image and synthesized his voice from newscasts and other sources. I've got the essential Beaumont stored on disk now. I can make him do anything I want."

Cris flipped another switch and the hologram began to speak. As it did so, the shoes on the holo-Beaumont undulated, rippled, and changed into seaweed.

"I'd like to tell you all about my new project, Pacifica," it said. The transformation continued up the legs and trunk. The seaweed took on an almost snakelike appearance, and the ends of the vine began nipping at and fighting with one another.

"It's my plan to save the world," said holo-Beaumont. The chest and arms disappeared into a mass of writhing kelp. "The sea can supply all the food we need." A strand of seaweed grew into Beaumont's mouth and he swallowed it. As he began sucking in the kelp like spaghetti, the lower part of the image began changing again, this time into stacks of money. "Beaumont Industries—we serve the world," boomed Beaumont's voice as the last of the kelp disappeared and the Beaumont-holo stood knee-deep in money.

"How do you like it?"

"Whew . . . are you really going to give that to Beaumont?" said Jill with a chuckle. "You know he's just going to throw it out."

"Perhaps," Cristopher sighed. "But at least he and Marica will see it, and that's enough for me."

"You use more than just lasers in something like that, right?"

Cris switched off the Beaumont holo and turned on another hologram.

A rainbow shimmered in the air before them, then slowly coalesced into a crowd of dancers. As they moved, he realized he'd chosen the wrong display, but it was too late and there was nothing he could do but continue.

"Most of my works combine sculpture and painting," he said, watching the swirling dancers. Twelve couples, men in tuxedos and tails, women in shimmering, sequinned glitter-dresses. Twelve Maricas and Twelve Cristophers, all madly in love, all dancing away the night while fireworks pinwheeled over their heads.

Jill stared at him. He scarcely noticed, caught up in the illusion, the twelve Maricas dancing around and around, their dresses swirling, their laughs echoing in his ears. His head hurt. He found he'd been holding his breath.

Abruptly, he switched off the dancers.

"It is beautiful," Jill said. "I didn't know you danced."

She twirled like one of the dancing Maricas, holding up the imaginary hem of an imaginary gown, laughing. From most women it would have seemed a sick parody of Marica, but somehow Jill made it work. She had a grace he hadn't expected.

Some leap of imagination made him picture her in a holo— her sarong soft and blue, her arms out-stretched in welcome to the world, her mouth lifting in a faint smile. It was the sea scene he'd sketched for Marica earlier, he realized, only tailored now to Jill. Not softer, not harder, just different.

He closed his eyes and saw the dark skin of Jill's shoulders glistening in the moonlight. Behind her the waves turned azure and silver.

He blinked the illusion away. She was smiling at him now, her soft lips half-parted. For a second he didn't know if he was really looking at her or not. When he reached out to touch her, to make sure, he felt skin as warm as the sun on sand. He squeezed her arm.

Then her head tilted up, and her eyes finally locked with his. They were the rich, dark brown of earth newly plowed.

They held pain and perhaps fear, he realized, though her face kept perfect calm.

"What's wrong?" he asked softly.

"Nothing." Those beautiful eyes flickered away from his, studying the paintings stacked against the walls, the mannequins painted with Marica's features, the tables piled with paints and brushes and cameras and mirrors—anything but him.

He took her face in his hands, leaning it back so that he could look deep into her eyes again. When she tried to pull away, he didn't let her. Tears welled up in her eyes, and she tried helplessly to stop them.

She needed him, he realized, and somehow, in his loneliness and despair, he needed her too. He kissed her softly, and it was good, so good. Only the present mattered, he thought. The world narrowed to just the two of them, and then to just her eyes, so dark and vulnerable.

When she kissed him back, hungrily, he pulled her to him, sweeping her up in his arms. It felt so good to touch a woman again. He pressed his lips against her cheeks, her ears, the curve of her neck—reveling in the scent of her, the softness of her body beneath his.

Her hands tugged at his shirt, unbuttoning it. He fumbled with her clothes as he tried to remove them. She giggled like a young girl and helped him.

Naked, she was even more beautiful, her breasts high and firm, her waist thin and tapered, her legs so long he thought they'd never end. He kissed her nipples erect while she tickled the hairs on his back, and then she moaned and pulled him down to her.

Somehow they made it to the bedroom. In the dark, they explored each other's bodies slowly and thoroughly, letting their passion grow to wild abandon. When they made love, it was short, but as intense as anything Cris had ever known.

Afterward, as they lay spooned together, he found Jill studying him. She smiled almost hesitantly, and he smiled back.

She hadn't expected they'd make love, he guessed, any more than he had.

"Why did you really come over?" he asked softly.

"To see you."

"No. I mean really."

"I . . . don't know. It seemed like the right thing to do, some- how." She cuddled a bit closer to him, her hand on his chest. It felt good, and he left it there and pulled her a little closer. "A.J. didn't need me tonight. He said I could take off if I wanted. I needed to get away from everyone and everything for a little while."

"Me too," he whispered. They had both needed closeness and comfort, he thought, though he didn't know where it would lead. She was vulnerable, the way Marica was, and like Marica, seemed to be purposefully hiding her secret thoughts from him.

Then, as his thoughts turned to Marica, he began to feel unclean, as though he'd betrayed her. *But it wasn't like that,* he thought. *She's the one who abandoned me.*

He couldn't help it, though. For a short while he had forgot- ten her, but now the specter of her presence rose again before him. In his mind's eye, he could hear her laughing, could see her dancing around and around like the holograms outside.

Jill must have sensed the change in him. Abruptly their bodies no longer seemed to fit together comfortably. She sat up and pulled on her bra and blouse.

"What is it?" Cris asked, and felt stupid as soon as the words escaped.

"Nothing," she said. "I just needed a friend tonight."

"Are you worried about your family?" She had told him about their struggle to hold onto their farm.

She hesitated a little too long and then said, "Yes."

He caught her arm as she reached for the rest of her clothes. "Are you sorry about what happened?"

"No, not at all." She smiled and leaned over to kiss him on the forehead. It felt good, but the passion had gone.

"Don't you be sorry, either," she said. "I'm a big girl. We both needed someone tonight, that's why it happened. We're just friends, that's all. I know you're still thinking about Marica."

Cris glanced away, embarrassed. He never should have let things go this far with Jill, he knew. He wasn't certain how she felt about him, but she seemed to feel more emotion than he could ever return. Why did he still want Marica? Why couldn't he control his emotions the way he wanted to?

He said, "Maybe once she marries Beaumont . . ."

"I hope so," said Jill. "For your sake. They *are* going to get married, and I don't think you could stop Beaumont even if you tried."

"I don't want to stop them," he said, almost bitterly. "She's just using him, you know, like she uses every man she meets. One more step up the social ladder for her."

He paused, thinking of Marica's layers of control and self-protection that formed a rigid shell shielding her from emotion. She had never talked about her childhood willingly, and if something slipped out inadvertently she quickly shifted away from the subject. He always sensed the hurt that lay beneath the surface, but he could never break through her armor.

"One more way of hiding from herself."

"You poor guy," said Jill, rubbing his shoulders. "You've got it bad, and from what I've seen, she's not worth it."

"That's what everyone says." Maybe he'd been fooling himself all along, he thought, thinking that Marica needed him, that she truly loved him, that she'd open up to him someday if he waited.

"If Marica's sticking it to Beaumont," Jill said, "it couldn't happen to a nicer guy."

"Think of the settlement she'll get when she divorces him."

Jill giggled. "That will take his highness down a peg or two." She continued dressing.

*   *   *

Only when she'd gone did Cris realize she hadn't told him about her problems. He should have pushed to help her. That's what a friend would do. That's what she'd done with him.

It *had* been good with her, he realized, better than with anyone except Marica. He felt all hollow inside thinking about it. And he vowed to see Jill again, no matter what it took, no matter what it cost him. That's what a friend would do.

Very alone, he curled around a pillow and tried to sleep.

Visions of Marica rose before him, her hands outstretched, beckoning.

ELEVEN

HEEJEES BUZZED around Beaumont's yacht like a swarm of angry bees. Since the *Lady Pecunia* had docked at one the fashionably trendy lower Manhattan piers for the wedding, it had fallen prey to City Control's bureaucratic computer-assisted dispatchers. Clearly, Jill thought as she listened to their half-panicked instructions on the public access band, the unusually heavy traffic flow to the wedding was wrecking havoc within the overcrowded heejee lanes.

And, to make matters worse, the dockside heejee landing strip had already filled to capacity. Those circling while they waited for clearance to land at any of the other nearby rooftop pads or garages further snarled air traffic.

Since she carried A.J. Beaumont, Jill should have had the greatest landing priority. However, City Control ordered her into the traffic circle, to wait with the masses of arriving guests.

"Control, you don't understand, this is Alexander James Beaumont's *personal* heejee."

She glanced back into the passenger compartment, where A.J. sat with his bodyguards. Luckily he was too busy instructing them on the wedding's security measures to bother her this trip. The bodyguards looked faintly ridiculous in their day-glo green tuxedos, but they'd blend with the Marica's glitterfolk friends. Only their thick, muscular necks and the slight bulges of their concealed guns would give them away. A.J. himself wore a tasteful, old-fashioned black tux. Its subtlety and reserve would make him stand out from the glitterfolk.

Then a dispatcher's ragged voice rasped in Jill's headphones: "I don't care who you are—get in line with the rest!"

If A.J. discovered his heejee was circling instead of landing, he'd have a fit.

Jill snapped back in the most officious tone she could muster, "Control, this is heejee GBI-One, we have Priority A-Zero-One." Beaumont had used his pull to get New York's Mayor Pollack to authorize the top priority for his wedding day. "Mr. Beaumont is on board. We are landing aboard the *Lady Pecunia* itself, not the parking strips for guests. We are landing *now.*"

The yacht's roof had a small helipad, big enough for several heejees. Marica Von-Grendel's oversized heejee already took up most of the space. Normally Jill would have thought twice before landing in such a small area, but she figured squeezing in was preferable to facing A.J.'s wrath if he discovered she'd been circling for half an hour.

She didn't wait for City Control to reply. With their state of confusion, it would take too long for them to clear her course. She took the heejee off autopilot and hit the button on her dashboard that warned her passengers of an impending landing. In the passenger section, a soft computer-generated voice said: "Please be seated, and please fasten your seat belts. We are about to land."

The heejee wheeled left, cutting out of the approach lane, and dropped through the circle of waiting vehicles. Barely skimming above the surface of the water, they zipped past the giant yacht. At the keel the heejee soared upward again, hovered for a moment, and then gently settled onto the rooftop landing pad. There was barely enough room between it and the Vonn-Grendel machine to open the pilot-side door.

Smiling with satisfaction, Jill shut down the motor, opened the other door for Beaumont, and pulled out the collapsible steps.

Oblivious to her tricky piloting, Beaumont hurried past without a word, followed by his two guards.

Jill slipped off her wireless earphones, ignoring City Control's curses. If they gave her a citation, one of the company's lawyers would take care of it, she thought. That was one of the few advantages of working for someone as powerful as Beaumont.

Exiting the heejee, she paused to look at the sky. Clouds brooded ominously overhead, a thick gray blanket with darker threads slipping quickly underneath. It would rain again, and soon, like so many other days. The clouds should have been in the south or midwest, where they needed it. October in New York: as warm and muggy as a summer's day. She couldn't remember the last time there'd been snow in the city.

The sky's gloom only heightened her own depression. She'd been waiting for the axe to fall ever since that day at the Green Age sweat lodge. She'd looked in a few trash cans for Pacifica papers, hoping they might satisfy Jade Moon, but hadn't found anything interesting. She hadn't even sent the bribe they'd given her to her parents. She'd put it into an envelope instead, addressed it to them, and then stuck it into her desk drawer. She felt as trapped as a rat waiting for the maze door to open, except that she knew this maze had no exit.

Last night Jade Moon had phoned her, demanding a meeting before the wedding at the yacht's helipad. Since she had nothing to give Jade, she had no idea whether the woman would follow through on her threat to turn over the holo-recording to Beaumont. She almost felt it would better to lose her job, at least then the tension would end. In any case, she had made up her mind that she was not going to go along with any terrorist plans, if that was what the Green Agers had in mind for her.

She looked around, but Jade Moon hadn't yet arrived. She was probably circling in the heejee jam.

Hearing footsteps coming from the other side of the landing pad, she hurried around the Vonn-Grendel heejee. Instead of Jade Moon, she found Cristopher.

"What are you doing here?" she asked in surprise. This was the last place she ever would have expected to see Cris. Certainly Beaumont would have gone out of his way to make sure no invitation had been sent to him.

His long hair had been neatly combed back and tied into a pony tail. He wore a brilliant azure-blue tuxedo to fit in with the glitterfolk guests.

"Marica sent me an invite. She couldn't miss the last chance to rub it in, I guess."

"You shouldn't have come."

Cris smiled wryly and nodded. Then he put his arm gently around her shoulder, the way a big brother would. "Thanks for your concern, but I'll be all right. I have to see her actually tie the knot with that bastard Beaumont before I'll really believe it. It's kind of like going to a funeral—you need to see the body before you can make yourself believe someone's dead."

"You're not going to cause any problems, are you? If Beaumont sees you he could have you tossed off the boat."

"No." Cris looked sad but calm. "I'll keep out of his way, stay in the back for the ceremony, then leave before the reception. Are you going to the wedding? That uniform of yours looks a little informal."

Jill glanced down at her blouse and pants. It wasn't an official uniform of any sort, Beaumont didn't like them, but the navy blue gave her a professional look that she found useful when piloting.

"I'm just the hired help, not a guest. I get to hang around until the bride and groom are ready to leave."

"Too bad. I could use the company. Moral support, you know."

"Maybe I should stick with you to keep you out of trouble, but unfortunately I have duties here." She glanced around anxiously; Jade Moon could arrive any minute.

Cris didn't seem to notice. "Beaumont's really making this wedding as lavish as possible," he said, glancing across the ship. "You should see the buffet they're setting up. They must've flown in a ton of fresh fish from Pacifica. People are rioting for bread in Chicago, and Beaumont's guests get more for dinner than most people see in a week." He sighed, staring out at the dismal gray day. "It isn't right."

"I think things will start late," Jill said. "Marica invited too many guests. The heejees are stacked up from here to Staten Island trying to land." She walked over to the edge of the helipad and scrutinized the crowd on the decks below, looking for Jade. "But hadn't you better be getting down there, in case something starts?"

"In a few minutes, just before the ceremony. I don't want to run into A.J." He followed her gaze. "Actually, I'm not sure I want to talk to any of those people."

The guests included an odd mix of Marica's glitterfolk friends and A.J.'s business contacts, who ranged from well-heeled investors, bankers, and lawyers; to suppliers, partners, and rivals; to politicians, movie stars, and famous intellectuals. In some instances the glitterfolk were the children of A.J.'s associates, although Marica was just a few years younger than A.J.

Only a few of the most prominent reporters had been invited. The rest of the press clustered at the land-end of the gangplank like a pack of hungry dogs, barking and snapping at each new arrival as they tried to get a quote or a photo.

The glitterfolk lived up to their name. Viewed from above, they looked like sparkling confetti. Some wore holofabrics projecting extravagant and eye-catching images they felt were suitable for the occasion of a wedding: African fertility dances, babies, pillars of fire. Others sported sequins, beads, or metallic fabrics. The older group included men in bright tuxedos and women in satin, taffeta, and lace.

Jill could almost feel their nervous excitement. They paced back and forth along the deck in a shifting pattern that seemed almost like a deliberate, serpentine dance. Whichever group they came from, the guests all had the same motive for being here. They wanted to see and be seen. This was the social event of the year; the place to make contacts and break them. Except for a few family members, probably nobody down there cared whether they'd come to a wedding or a funeral. And some doubtless didn't know. She couldn't blame Cristopher for not wanting to mingle with them.

Yet somehow she found the whole thing entertaining to watch, though it really *was* rather repulsive. No matter how bad the world got, the rich could always be found living it up at extravagant parties and celebrating meaningless events, like this obviously loveless marriage.

She could picture her mother at home in her tiny kitchen, trying to wipe away the dust that never stopped sifting into the house, no matter how solidly closed the doors and windows were. It formed a continuous layer of grime which her toil never completely removed. She could imagine her dad outside, trying to plow fields of dust instead of dirt, stubbornly refusing to give in to defeat, even though he had already lost his war years ago.

Like most of the people of the world, they struggled to survive amidst poverty and famine. They represented reality. This party and these guests were dreams. And as usual, the rich in their shadow world neither knew nor cared what happened outside their own small corner of the universe.

Perhaps Cris really wasn't any better than the rest, though at least his obsession was for a person rather than power and money. Jill doubted that Marica's marriage could free him from her spell. She glanced over at him and wondered why Marica had ever let him go. *She must really be as stupid as she acts,* she thought, *to exchange Cris for Beaumont.*

"I'd better get down there," he finally said.

Jill noticed the crowd starting to move into the yacht's salon, where the actual ceremony would take place. Servants began setting up more long tables for the reception buffet. She wondered how they managed to get such a variety of food, even from the black market.

"Please take it easy," she told him.

"Don't worry about me. I'm fine."

As she watched the big man trot down the stairs and disappear into the crowds below, she hoped he really *was* as much in control as he seemed. She hated to think what would happen if he and Beaumont started a fist-fight again.

It started to drizzle, but it was so warm out that the wetness hardly bothered her. Below, crewmen pulled awnings over the bow to protect the guests.

She began to pace back and forth between the two heejees. What had happened to Jade Moon? Jade had been quite adamant that they meet.

"You Washington?" a voice called behind her.

"Yes?" She turned.

A young, dark-skinned man came up the stairs. He looked tall, well-built, and fairly muscular, and the tips of his black, curly hair had been dyed bright green. He wore a knee-length holo-robe over black slacks. A golden cornfield rippled over his body and part of the way into the air around him.

"Jade Moon sent me," he said. He pulled a pendant from beneath his shirt and waved it toward her like a calling card: a hologram of the Earth locked inside a black crystal. She'd seen one like it before—on Harrison.

"I'm Redwood," he said.

She couldn't help but smile at his Green Age name. "Where's Jade?"

"Down at the wedding. She's the Maid of Honor."

"I know, but she asked me to meet her here."

"She sent me instead, to make sure you wait for her until after the ceremony."

Jill shrugged. "You can just tell her . . ." She hesitated, trying to think of an innocuous message, since she knew nothing about this guy Redwood. "Tell her nothing's new with me. I don't need to see her today."

"*She* wants to see you." Redwood's voice suddenly had a nasty edge. Jade Moon's instructions were a command, it seemed, not a request. "I'm your company until she gets here," he went on. "Why don't we wait inside the heejee? We're getting wet."

The drizzle had gotten heavier, threatening to become a steady rain.

Something about Redwood's attitude made Jill nervous. He didn't seem like one of the usual airheaded glitterfolk. His accent spoke more of the inner city than the social set. He looked the part, but his jittery arrogance reminded her of a street punk.

"I'll be here," she said slowly. "You can tell Jade that I'll wait for her. After all, you don't want to miss the wedding."

Redwood snorted, and his face looked older and more sinister. "I don't care about that crap. I'm supposed to wait here, with you. Jade Moon wants you ready to pilot the heejee if she needs it. So don't go getting any fancy ideas. I'll be here with you the whole time."

"Sure." Jill looked around uneasily. Everything felt wrong. After the wedding she was supposed to fly the 'happy couple' to their honeymoon 'cabin'—an isolated 20-room mansion in Maine. As Maid of Honor, Jade must have known that. So what was Redwood talking about?

"Let's get in outta the rain, huh?" He gestured firmly toward A.J.'s heejee.

The downpour had gotten heavy enough that Jill had become uncomfortable. Reluctantly she climbed into the heejee with Redwood right behind. She glanced back at him with distaste. *Why was he here? What was Jade Moon up to?*

TWELVE

"THESE FLOWERS are all wrong!" Marica shouted, throwing the bouquet to the floor. The wedding music would start at any moment, signaling the start of the ceremony, but everything was going wrong. She hated the roses.

Picking up the bouquet, Jade Moon examined it carefully, preening the deep red roses back into perfect alignment. "What's wrong with it? It *is* beautiful."

"I wanted something simple and natural—it's all plastic— it's hateful!" Marica felt flustered and confused, not certain why the bouquet made her so angry.

"It's just a plastic base to hold the flowers in place. The flowers are real."

"I *hate* it!" Tears welled up in her eyes. She felt her face turning red with anger. She didn't know whether she wanted to laugh or to cry. The plastic holder did bother her, but there was more too it than that. *Roses.*

"She's just having wedding jitters," said Laurie Ann Beaumont, A.J.'s aunt. "It happens all the time."

Not at my weddings, Marica thought. After all, it was her fifth, and no different than any of the others, she tried to tell herself. But in the back of her mind she knew that it *was* different, and all because of Cris.

The roses had reminded her of him. As much as she tried to deny it, she knew he'd been the only one she had truly loved. And having let herself love, she'd lost control. She'd become as vulnerable as the men she hoped to dominate.

Laurie Ann prattled on in her annoying Southern whine. "Why, I remember when I got married for the first time. I could hardly keep from faint'n dead away, right in the middle of the ceremony! My husband, Billy Lee, said I looked white as a sheet. Then cousin Martha, she just up and flew into a rage 'cause she didn't want to wear a garter, even though it was the only blue thing she had to wear, and of course you *must* wear something blue, you know. You have something blue, haven't you my dear?"

"No," said Marica, just to be perverse. But like almost every other bride that had ever existed she had bowed to the superstitions. Not that she believed in them. However, a marriage needed all the help it could get, and one honored the old superstitions on the chance that they might actually do some good.

"Oh my goodness, how awful! You must wear something blue."

"Why?" Marica found it hard to keep a straight face at the old biddy's obvious distress.

"Why?" The old woman looked confused. "Well, you have to, that's all." She began rummaging through her purse. "I *must* have something blue I can give you, and something old, and . . ."

"That's all right, Mrs. Beaumont. Marica already has something blue, and all the rest too," said Jade Moon.

Marica began to laugh.

A low chime sounded outside.

"That's the signal! It's almost time for the ceremony!" said Laurie Ann. "Are you sure you have everything, honey?""Yes, Laurie Ann." Marica felt as though she were talking to a small child. "See the bracelet—new and blue." She held up the sapphire bracelet A.J. had given her as a wedding present. Its matched set of oval stones held the deep blue of the evening sky. "Jade lent me an old lace handkerchief, too."

"Thank goodness," said the old lady with a hearty sigh. "You were just teasing me, weren't you child? Land of mercy!"

"What are you going to do about the flowers?" asked Jade. Her face, as always, was painted bright green, and her miniskirted, strapless frock was exactly the same shade.

Marica still disliked them, but her hysteria had changed from a temper tantrum into the frantic urge to laugh. With an effort of will she stifled her panic. "It's too late to get anything different now. Give them here."

Jade patted her shoulder. "Don't worry, Marica, you're going to love being married to A.J. He's got all these fabulous yachts, and villas all around the world, and anything else you could possibly want. You're going to have the best time of your life."

Marica felt her composure beginning to return. Jade was so supportive. If it weren't for her, Marica might never have gotten involved with A.J. at all.

"Am I a mess?" she asked, turning to stare at herself in the floor-length mirror of the stateroom. She patted her cheeks to make sure her makeup remained undisturbed.

"You look fine," said Laurie Ann. "Just beautiful."

Marica smoothed the knee-length skirt of her gown. Peacock blue silk, it matched her eyes perfectly. She twirled, studying the fabric against her skin. The low-cut back and bodice revealed enough to entice without stepping over the boundary to tastelessness. The designer, DiNucci, had outdone himself this time, creating a frock that at first glance made her look youthful and innocent, but when she walked, clung to her frame sensuously.

She tugged at the small headpiece. It held a neck-length veil, now lifted back so her face remained uncovered. It seemed lopsided, always slipping down, and the more she fussed with it, the worse it looked.

"Leave it alone, will you?" exclaimed Jade. She adjusted Marica's headpiece once again, pulling the veil down over Marica's face.

The door flew open suddenly, and a young woman leaned inside. "The music is starting," she called.

Just then Marica heard it, the first strains of the traditional wedding march. Her hands felt cold and clammy. She swallowed. Nervousness always hit her just before the ceremony. Today it seemed far worse. She tried not to think of Cris.

Laurie Ann hurried out.

"Here we go," said Jade. She held the door open for Marica.

Putting on her best smile and a vapid, dewy-eyed look, Marica strutted after her like a cover-girl model. Turning, she headed down the corridor and up the steps into the yacht's main salon.

Faces blurred through the veil. The music swelled. Flashes from cameras began to go off as she entered the lounge.

Intent on her appearance, Marica hardly noticed. She had to watch her step to keep in time to the music, she had to tilt her head at just the right angle so the ceiling lights would hit her face without casting ugly shadows, and she had to keep her smile warm and receptive without letting it seem false or rehearsed. She didn't know any more whether she concentrated on all these little tricks to look her best or just to keep her mind from thinking too deeply, exposing her to hurtful memories.

A.J. stood before the Mayor of New York, Thomas Pollack, who would conduct the ceremony. He grinned at Marica like a little boy finding a bright red bicycle beneath the Christmas tree.

She smiled back, but felt no emotion. Beaumont himself meant nothing to her. He was just a tool she could use, a prize she had won. Strangely, she didn't feel the triumph she'd expected for snaring him. She felt empty inside.

She barely heard Mayor Pollack say "We are gathered together to unite this man and this woman in marriage."

In her mind's eye she saw Cris's face turn pale the moment she had announced her engagement. She didn't dare look around to see if he'd accepted her invitation to come. Now she felt sorry and ashamed that she'd sent it. She hated herself for trying to torment him.

"Do you, Marica Vonn-Grendel, take Alexander James Beaumont to love and to cherish, to honor and to comfort, in sickness or in health, in sorrow and in joy, to have and to hold from this day forth?"

Mayor Pollack looked at her expectantly.

Marica heard herself say, "I do."

She felt as though she were two people, one the driven, animated part that always had to be in control, that couldn't let her guard down, that wouldn't get hurt again no matter what happened. The other side was the part she thought she'd destroyed long ago, the part that needed love, the part that had been betrayed, the little girl lost. That second side of herself should have been dead by now, it had been buried so deep and so long. Yet it kept creeping back to life.

I'm in command. she thought. *I'm the strong one. There's just me, and I've got what I want.*

"By the power vested in me by the State of New York, I pronounce you man and wife. You may kiss the bride."

A.J. gave her a lengthy kiss. Then he triumphantly took her arm and escorted her back down the aisle.

They'd barely gotten outside the door when the guests began to surround them, giving their congratulations.

Two faces came sharply into focus among the throng. She hadn't seen the two in so long that for a moment she wasn't sure they were really who she thought they were—the people she hoped never to see again. They pushed forward, pressing in, *surrounding* her.

Marica shook her head and tried to back away. There were too many people, and these two reached for her, tried to hug her to them.

"Sweetheart—"

"My baby. . ."

"No, get away." Marica felt as though she were screaming, but her voice croaked out the words hardly above a whisper.

Their arms were around her, pulling her to them. She felt suffocated. The man hugged her, arms brushing her breasts through her gown. He smelled of stale tobacco and licorice breath-mints that tried to conceal the stench of alcohol.

Recoiling, Marica grabbed A.J.'s arm.

"My parents!" she yelled, and this time her voice was a bellow that turned heads and silenced those around them. "You promised me you wouldn't invite them!"

"I thought it would be a nice surprise."

"I don't *want* them here!"

A.J.'s face reddened. "Not so loud. What's the matter?"

"I told you not to invite them," she said urgently in his ear. The guests were still staring at her, wondering what was going on.

Her father pushed close again, trying to hold her. "Susan, how lovely you are."

She flinched and backed away. Where he'd touched her, her skin seemed to burn as though he had struck it.

"Damn you, get away from me!" she yelled, slapping at his arms. Her stomach twisted, and she felt sick.

"Sue—what *ever* is the matter with you?" said her mother. She half-turned away to address no one in particular and at the same time all the guests that were nearby. "She never knows how to behave. She always thinks she's better than everyone else—even her name isn't good enough, Susan's too common, so we all have to call her Marica. But I refuse to call her by that ridiculous name."

"A.J.—get—them—*out*—*of*—*here!*" Marica fought to get back into control.

He looked at her with disgust. "Get a grip on yourself," he

whispered. "These are your parents, and even if you don't like them you can be civil to them. Think of our other guests."

"It's been so long," said her father. What was left of his balding hair was dyed jet black. Deep lines etched his face like crevices. "It was nice of you to invite us."

"I didn't invite you, you goddamn son of a bitch!"

Her father turned purple. Her mother's mouth dropped open. A.J. grimaced, and the glitterfolk crammed in closer.

"Please excuse her," A.J. said to all the onlookers. "Just a little family disagreement."

Marica could hear Laurie Ann's southern drawl in the crowd. "It's wedding nerves, that's all. Just before the ceremony she threw her bouquet on the ground and stomped around makin' quite a fuss!"

"They go or I do!" she howled.

A.J. ignored her. Turning to her parents he said, "Why don't you help yourself to the buffet? I'm sure it's just jitters, and Marica's going to cool off shortly."

"Damn you!" Marica's face felt as hot as flame.

Her mother clutched her arm. The years had changed her, making her face softer and more frail-looking, though plastic surgery kept most of her beauty intact. Her strawberry-blond hair hung loosely down her back like a young girl's.

"It's about time you invited me to one of your weddings— you've had enough of them."

"I didn't invite you!" Marica pried her mother's fingers away. "I told you before, and I still mean it. I never want to see either of you again."

She wrenched away from them and rammed through the crowd to the corridor. Tears streamed down her cheeks, and she couldn't stop them, couldn't still the wild pounding of her heart.

Behind her she could hear A.J. trying to soothe her parents' feelings. She didn't care. She never wanted to see any of them again.

She fled down the steps, barely able to see them, and sagged against the wall by her stateroom.

Why had he asked them to come? She couldn't understand it. She hadn't expected them, and the shock had torn through the defenses she'd built over the years.

She felt ten years old again, powerless to help herself.

She banged her head against the wall, as she used to do, over and over again, waiting for the pain to help block out the present.

Someone grabbed her and pulled her away.

"No!" She lashed out, fighting him, never wanting him to touch her again.

"Marica. Marica. Please."

He held her against his body, cushioning her with it.

The hands stroking her were big hands. The voice filled with concern comforted rather than humiliated.

It wasn't her father.

"Cristopher?" she gasped through sobs. He'd followed her from the deck.

"I'm here," he whispered. "Everything's going to be fine."

"Leave me alone," she cried, ashamed. Ducking away from him, she ran to her stateroom.

He came in after her, before she could close the door. She flailed wildly at him, trying to push him away. But he wouldn't move, just stood there and let her hit him. Finding no resistance, Marica collapsed against him, crying.

The barriers she'd worked so hard to build seemed to have vanished. Her emotions commanded her, twisting her calmness into rage, turning her from the master of her fate into a helpless victim. A victim she'd sworn never to be again.

Cristopher stroked her hair in silence, until her sobs gradually became sniffles.

"Why do you put up with me?" she asked him finally. "Why do you waste your time with me?"

"You know why, Marica. I've loved you since the first day we met."

She remembered that day. She'd felt worthless and alone and had gone to the museum to lose herself among the beauty. She'd seen Cris's holograms and had been entranced. The purity of his vision had intrigued her—fields of wheat, glistening in the sun; a marching line of ants; a simple rose. Somehow, they caught the essence of her childhood, the early years when they lived in the country. The days when she'd been a little girl and happy. The days before her father began to drink too heavily. The time before the violence and pain.

"Marica," he said softly, "what got you so upset? I heard you yelling at your parents. I knew you didn't get along, but the way you pushed your father away . . . ?"

"I hate him."

Cris lifted her chin, studying her face as though seeing it for the first time.

"You seemed repelled by his touch."

She couldn't meet his probing gaze.

"God, Marica, it never occurred to me before—did he molest you?"

She felt the shame coloring her face crimson. She had tried so hard to forget those days.

"He did, didn't he?"

She nodded and clung to him.

"Your mother . . . why didn't she stop it? Didn't you tell her?"

"I told her. She didn't believe me—she didn't want to believe me. When I got older though, she saw things, and she knew. She said he was a good provider. She said I shouldn't talk about it. She said she didn't want to hear about it. She was afraid he'd beat her more if she complained."

The words came out in jagged clumps, each sentence harder than the next to say, harder to reveal. Yet when she finished, she felt better for having said them, for letting Cris see past the walls she'd built.

"You should have told me before," he said. "You should have let me help you. You've been keeping all this pain inside where it only hurts you more."

She pressed against him. "It's driven me away from you, Cris. I didn't want to love you, but I couldn't help myself."

He kissed her forehead. As his hands caressed her, her skin tingled. This was the way it had always been between them, the reason he had scared her so much. She'd been afraid to let herself feel passion, to yield to him, to love him. She was still afraid. But for the first time her need for him and his love was greater than her fear.

"I love you," she said, looking up into his face, into his eyes. For the first time, when she said those words aloud, she really meant them.

She melted in his arms, feeling truly a part of him. The part of her that demanded control, that had to dominate to avoid domination, was still afraid, but it was no longer too afraid to trust.

She would never let him go again.

Suddenly there was a knock on the door.

She and Cris looked at one another.

"You're not going with Beaumont," said Cris.

"No, I'm not," said Marica. "I'll tell him it's over between us." She smiled at how short their marriage had lasted. She'd made many mistakes in her life, but for once she wasn't going to make another one.

She opened the door. Jade Moon stood there, with an older, heavy-set man named Forrest, whom Marica had met once or twice.

"What are you doing here?" Jade asked Cris, pushing her way into the room.

"I—" Marica found she didn't know how to answer.

"Never mind," said Jade, apparently sensing something amiss as she looked back and forth between them. "I'm here to help you get out of that wedding dress and into your traveling clothes. Cristopher, you'd better leave now.""Something happened, Jade," Marica said. "I've realized I don't love A.J. This marriage was a mistake. I need to speak to him right away."

Marica headed for the door.

"Forrest," said Jade Moon, "close that."

Forrest slammed the door shut as Marica reached for the handle. Marica turned with a questioning look.

Jade reached into the purse dangling from her wrist and pulled out a gun. Though small, it had a silencer on the barrel. Forrest also took out a gun. He aimed his squarely at Cris.

"What's going on?" Cris looked as confused as Marica felt.

"Marica, you're coming with us."

"What are you talking about?" she demanded. She felt a wave of panic wash over her like winter rain. "Jade—"

"Beaumont's been lying to you about Pacifica," said Jade. "He's not planning to feed the whole world, just those who can pay for it. And as for using the ocean a source of energy, that's a publicity gimmick. He owns too many oil fields and too many pollution-control companies. He's happy with the famine.

That's what makes his kelp so valuable."

"Even if that's true," said Cris, "what's Marica got to do with it?"

"We've been trying to get his plans and bacteria for months, but we haven't been able to."

"You're part of this `Green Action Now!' group, right?" asked Cris. "Harrison was one of your men."

"The Earth is our mother, we must protect her," said Forrest. "We are only doing what we have to do."

"But what have I got to do with that?" said Marica, staring fixedly at Forrest's gun.

Jade Moon's expression remained unreadable through her mask of green. "I'm sorry to involve you in this, but you're A.J.'s wife now, and he'll do anything to keep you safe. I'm afraid we're going to have to kidnap you. A.J. will give us the bacteria to get you back. We have no other choice."

"Cristopher, put your hands above your head," she said with a nod toward Forrest. "We don't want to hurt you, but the world is more important than any one man."

"You won't get off this yacht with all these people around," said Cris.

"We'll worry about that," said Forrest. "Do as you're told." The heavy-set man motioned at Cris with his gun.

Cris slowly raised his arms.

"Now turn around," ordered Forrest.

Cris looked anxiously at Marica.

"Do it," said Jade Moon. "Don't worry about Marica. She's our insurance policy. We'll be taking good care of her."

Marica felt as though she couldn't breathe. Cris slowly turned toward the wall.

Forrest stepped close behind Cris. Then he slammed his pistol hard against Cris's head.

"Oh God!" Marica cried, running toward him. As he hit the floor she could see blood on his scalp.

"No you don't," said Jade, grabbing her arm and twisting her around. She pressed the muzzle of her gun into Marica's stomach. Marica couldn't believe this was the same woman she'd known and called a friend. "Let's go!"

Forrest opened the cabin door and peeked out. "All clear."

Jade pushed her roughly through the doorway. They hurried down the corridor to the aft elevator. Its door had been wedged open with a fire extinguisher. Then Jade Moon shoved her inside and hit the button for the helipad. Forrest kicked the fire extinguisher out of the way.

As the elevator doors closed, Marica saw Cris stagger from the stateroom, blood dripping from the hand he held pressed to his head.

THIRTEEN

CRISTOPHER LEANED against the stateroom door, dazed. He'd felt the blow coming and tried to move his head when Forrest had hit him; so the blow merely grazed his scalp, tearing skin and not doing any major damage. Still, it hurt like hell.

He reached the corridor in time to see the elevator doors close. Most of the guests were at the reception in the ship's bow. Apparently Jade Moon had used the aft elevator to avoid detection. Cris shook his head, confused. It didn't seem possible that she'd kidnap Marica right in the middle of the wedding.

He pushed himself after them, but of course the elevator had gone. Ramming his hand against the call button, he wondered if he should go to the reception for help. But with the crowds of guests and confusion, it would take so much time that Jade Moon would probably get away.

Why was the elevator taking so long? He pounded on the call button in frustration. Then he stepped back and looked at the lighted numbers over the elevator.

They'd gone to the roof—the heliport. He started for the stairs, but the ache in his head made him dizzy and he had to stop a moment. Leaning against the wall, pressing his eyes closed, he tried not to throw up. *I must be hurt worse than I thought,* he decided.

It seemed to take forever for the elevator to arrive. He couldn't just stand there, so he paced, almost tripping over the fire extinguisher they'd used to keep the doors open. Then he picked it up thoughtfully. Perhaps he could use it as a weapon.

The kidnapping still didn't make a whole lot of sense to him. Why kidnap Marica now? Certainly, as Marica's alleged best friend, Jade Moon would have had better opportunities before—or even after—the ceremony.

She must've been waiting for the wedding to get as much leverage as possible against Beaumont. Marica was Beaumont's wife now. Beaumont would have to meet their demands.

The elevator finally arrived. Cris jumped inside. Mirrored walls passed his reflection back and forth, an infinity of mocking images. The blood on his face, the lights in his eyes—he swayed as he punched the heliport's button.

How can this be happening? For a moment it seemed he'd found Marica again. Perhaps he'd seen the real woman inside for the first time, without any pretense or barrier between them. *I have to get her back.*

The elevator stopped at the top floor. It felt like an eternity had passed. "You have reached the helideck," announced an annoying computer-generated voice.

As the doors opened, Cris tensed, ready to attack anyone on the other side. The little observation booth was deserted.

He careened out, not quite steady on his feet. He touched his face and his hand came away red. Blood trickled down his cheek, he realized, like a steady stream of tears. He gripped the fire extinguisher tightly, as he fought for control. *I have to help Marica.* The thought of her danger spurred him on.

A huge plate glass window looked out on the helipad. He pressed up against it, peering out. Marica's cumbersome heejee sat there, in the pouring rain, looking like an immense toad.

He hurried through a set of glass doors and onto the deck. Rain fell in sheets, soaking him. Ducking, he ran to the heejee and peered inside. *Empty.*

Then he heard raised voices from its other side. Remembering how Jill had parked over there, he eased to the left, using the heejee for cover. Carefully he peered around its tail.

Marica stood in front of Jill's smaller heejee, with Forrest right beside her, pointing his gun at her head. Cris shivered, uneasy, unwilling to rush them just yet. He didn't want Forrest shooting Marica by accident.

Jade Moon leaned against the open cockpit door, talking to the two people inside: Jill Washington and a young black man he'd seen once or twice with Jade at Marica's parties.

"You better cooperate," she said. "Don't forget that holo we have. You wouldn't want Beaumont seeing it, would you? And if that's not enough, think about that revolver Redwood's pointing at you. Think hard."

"Get in," Forrest ordered Marica, shoving her inside.

Cris pulled the fire extinguisher's safety pin, raised the nozzle, and sprinted forward. He didn't think, he acted, all the pent-up emotions pouring out at once, all the fear and anger and frustration and love.

He sprayed foam at Forrest's head. Forrest shrieked as the

acidic froth burned his face.

The heavy-set man spun around, shooting blindly at Cris. The shots went wild as the foam covered his eyes and nose.

Jade Moon dove into the heejee, yelling, "Take it up, take it up!"

The heejee lifted.

Forrest tottered, unable to see through the foam, and stumbled sideways. The heejee's tail swung around and clipped his side, knocking him off his feet. His gun sailed across the deck floor toward Cris.

Cris sprayed the foam at the heejee's cockpit. The rotor's down-draft blew most of the froth back at him, and then the rest fell short as the vehicle rose and veered away.

Staggering to his feet, Forrest lurched toward Cris. Cris aimed the foam at him and kept spraying. Forrest reeled backwards to the railing, crashed into it, and began climbing over it to escape the foam. Losing his balance, he pitched forward, falling into the ocean.

Cris flung the nearly empty canister away in disgust. Grabbing Forrest's gun, he squinted into the rain. Jill's heejee was too far away to hit, even if he dared risk a shot.

There was nothing to do except follow them. He tried the door to Marica's oversized heejee but found it locked. He pulled on the handle frantically. Then he fired the gun into the lock, destroying it.

Once inside, he quickly lifted the heejee from the *Lady Pecunia*'s deck. As it rose, he could see some of the guests and A.J.'s security men climbing the stairs to the helipad, apparently attracted by the gunfire.

He slipped on the radio's headphones. New York Control was trying to contact the Beaumont heejee that Jill flew.

"City Control," he called urgently. "This is PCX-440. This is an emergency!"

Jill's voice cut in. "This is Beaumont Industries' Heejee GBI-One. We have priority A-One-Zero. We are transporting Alexander James Beaumont and his wife for their honeymoon. Priority A-One-Zero, as authorized by Mayor Pollack. Please verify."

She headed at full-speed across Manhattan during rush hour, crossing dense traffic lanes.

"Heejee GBI-One, you have clearance."

"Control!" Cris said again, practically shouting. "This is PCX-440. Please contact police. Heejee GBI-One has been hijacked. Marica Vonn-Grendel—" he paused, hating to say the words. "Beaumont—the new Mrs. Beaumont has been kidnapped. Please check with the yacht *Lady Pecunia*. I am in pursuit."

"PCX-440, you do not have clearance. Return to regular traffic lanes. Police will check out your story."

"You goddamn *idiots*!" muttered Cris to himself, knowing that City Control's red tape would leave him circling while Beaumont's heejee disappeared in the heavy East Coast traffic. He decided to bluff it out.

"Central Control, I do not copy." He tapped a fingernail against the microphone at his throat. "I don't read you—bad reception—" He switched off the transmitter.

As the Maid of Honor, Jade Moon must have known about the heejee's high priority status, Cris realized. She'd probably planned on using it make their getaway.

And Jill Washington was a damn good pilot, he had to admit as he tried to follow her. She dropped in and out of traffic lanes, trying to lose herself in the flow. Jill obviously knew he pursued them. Flying in the metropolitan areas without computer control required both skill and daring, even with the heejee's built-in sensors to help locate other vehicles. That was dangerous enough. But it was almost suicidal to fly the way Jill did, cutting in and out of the regular lanes. Obviously she was an extraordinarily talented pilot.

He didn't really remember her from the days when she'd been one of his Air Force students. That had been about the time he'd decided to quit the Force, when he'd been assigned to the classroom. But he'd seen enough of Jill's flying to know she must've been one of the best in her class.

They'd pulled a gun on her, so they had to be forcing her to fly them. But did she have to be so darn efficient? He wondered why she'd taken her heejee off autopilot control. Surely the kidnappers weren't that well-versed in regular heejee operation. If she'd only fly like an average pilot, he thought, the police could use computer control to take over and land her heejee. All they'd need would be Beaumont's report of the kidnapping.

Why didn't Jill just let it happen?

The Beaumont heejee continued to pull away from him. Even taking the risks Jill did, the Vonn-Grendel heejee was too big, too bulky to keep up with her smaller craft for long.

Cris glanced down at the control panel, remembering the time last time he'd flown it. This model of helijet came equipped with expensive, non-standard holo-projectors. Perhaps, he thought, he could use them to fool Jill. If she thought she'd lost him, she might merge into the regular traffic flow to keep from drawing police attention. And that would give him his chance.

He let his heejee lag farther behind. In the rain, visibility was poor. Finally, dropping into one of the traffic lanes, he flipped on the holos, turning his heejee into something that looked like a South American tramp steamer. He hoped she hadn't noticed. Only a few other heejees in the traffic used projectors, and most of those were taxis that had turned themselves into advertisements—flying hamburgers, deodorants, tofu nutribars.

For the moment, Cris could still follow Jill's heejee on his radar. He'd had his computer flag it the moment he'd taken off; that was pretty routine, since the glitterfolk often traveled in groups of ten or more heejees. Jill had completely crossed Manhattan and now headed south along the Jersey Corridor lanes.

Cris accelerated, rising to the faster-moving top level of his lane. Manhattan Control had apparently given up trying to contact him since he'd reported radio trouble. They'd probably decided to track his course and leave it to the police to ticket him once he landed. He might lose his license for driving at non-priority speeds, but he really didn't care. If it happened, he'd appeal and claim his head injury left him momentarily deranged.

Thinking of that, he realized he felt much better. He touched his scalp gingerly; the blood had stopped flowing.

He began to review his options. Unless a heejee was on autopilot, it would be difficult to force it to land, so police generally waited for speeders to refuel or return home to pick them up. Since all heejees had built-in chips that tagged them for satellite monitoring, they could be operated by computer networks while on autopilot, allowing them to fly safely in the crowded lanes. This system also allowed police to monitor traffic code violations and track offenders. So the police probably wouldn't stop him until he caught up with Jill's heejee.

Cris sliced over to Jersey illegally, and dived below normal traffic lanes to go faster. He got a little too close to a low-flying heejee, and it slued to one side as it caught the brunt of his jetstream. He glimpsed several screaming women inside when he passed within a foot of its passenger cabin.

Jill's heejee had merged into regular traffic going at slower speeds. He could see it now: above and to the right, a dark blur against the rain and the clouds. Since she no longer had visual contact with him, she thought she'd lost him. He grinned; he hadn't taught *everything* he knew in those Air Force classes.

He began scanning radio frequencies. Strangely, none carried a report of the kidnapping. The Beaumont heejee still traveled with its priority clearance.

Cristopher almost felt sorry for A.J.—his wedding party ruined, his bride snatched. And if he got her back . . . *when* he got her back . . . he'd still lose her.

That was one thing Cristopher knew with certainty. Marica was his again. She really loved him. They would make their love work this time. She was going to be all right. She *had* to be.

The back of his head began to throb. He'd charged after Marica without much thought. He began to wonder what he'd do if he did catch up with them. He certainly couldn't shoot it out with Jade and the other GANs; he might hit Marica or Jill. All he could do was follow and hope to radio their position to the police. Undoubtedly Beaumont had reported the kidnapping by now; maybe the police were keeping it quiet to surprise the kidnappers.

Slowly he settled into the monotony of flying. He kept to a course paralleling the smaller heejee's; it seemed to be headed for Philadelphia. He coaxed his ponderous vehicle along at full throttle, barely keeping up. The big heejee had large power demands and not enough solar cells to meet them, and the auxiliary engine began running low on kerosine.

As he sat there, helpless to do more than watch and wait, his anger and frustration grew. The kidnapping played over and over again in his mind.

I should've done something differently. I should've jumped Forrest the moment he pulled a gun. I should never have let Marica go through with the wedding in the first place.

Finally, confident Jill wasn't going to get away for the moment, Cris switched over to autopilot. When he bent over and pulled the first aid kit from under his seat, his head throbbed anew. Gingerly he explored the scalp wound with his fingers; swelling made it hard to tell the extent of the wound.

He pulled a gauze and alcohol from the kit and began to clean up. Blood had clotted along the back of his head and dried on his cheek. He wiped it off and tried to clean the wound as best he could. It seemed basically superficial, a long raw cut along the back of his head.

Jill's heejee dipped unexpectedly, shifting into a landing pattern.

Cris flicked off autopilot and punched up a local map on the heejee's computer. He'd reached the fringes of northeast Philadelphia, a maze of twisting streets left over from the age before helijets caught on. If he didn't act fast, he might lose Jill among the buildings.

He gunned the engine, using every bit of his skill to catch up. He barely caught sight of them as they landed. Apparently the holographic projection still fooled them, since they made no evasive moves.

Following them in, he signaled Philadelphia City Control, once again reporting the kidnapping and describing the heejee's present location.

"Your information is in error," said the City Control dispatcher in a bored voice. "Your earlier report was routed to the police. Mr. Alexander Beaumont has been contacted aboard his yacht, and he does not, I repeat *does not* confirm any kidnapping."

"That's impossible," Cris said. But he'd begun to wonder . . . if Beaumont had been contacted by the kidnappers, they could've warned him not to go to the police.

"GBI-One has still has valid A-One-Zero priority," City Control said. "Since your radio is now working, you are instructed to land immediately. A police helijet is on its way."

"That's better!" Cris said.

"You have violated several of the Helijet Control Ordinances of Pennsylvania," the dispatcher went on.

"Oh great," Cris muttered.

The Beaumont Industry heejee landed at the corner of Castor Avenue and Magee. Small businesses lined the bigger avenue, while row houses ran along Magee. Cris couldn't see a public helipad anywhere nearby; he knew he'd have to land carefully, since old-style electrical lines still ran along both sides of the streets. His larger heejee wouldn't be able to land in the street as they had. He started looking and finally spotted an empty playground a block away.

He maneuvered the big craft down. It reacted sluggishly, like a bear coming out of hibernation. The holo projection still made it look like a South American banana boat—an unlikely sight for the middle of a children's playground, between a swing set and a jungle gym.

He grabbed Forrest's gun and headed back toward Castor Avenue. Somehow, he'd save Marica, he vowed.

By the time he rounded the corner, though, an old-fashioned black limousine had pulled up in front of Jill's heejee. Cris began to run. Jade Moon was dragging Marica across the street toward the limo. Ropes bound Marica's hands behind her back, and a scarf gagged her mouth. She struggled and fought, trying to get free without success.

Then she saw Cris and froze, staring. Jade Moon saw him too and raised her pistol to Marica's head. Cris skidded to a halt.

"Drop your gun!" Jade Moon called. "Do it, or I'll shoot her!"

Cris hesitated. He knew they wanted Marica as a hostage; she wouldn't do much good dead. Yet as Jade Moon trained her gun at Marica, he was afraid to move. Too much might go wrong. Reluctantly, he dropped Forrest's pistol to the ground and raised his hands.

Jade grinned triumphantly.

The limo's rear door limo opened and a skinny man in a green robe climbed out. He grabbed Marica and pulled her, screaming, into the car.

Meanwhile, the young black man, Redwood, had climbed out of Jill's heejee. He moved his aim from Jill to Cris and began edging his way toward the limo.

Realizing her opportunity while Redwood was distracted, Jill reached under the dashboard and silently pulled out the semi-automatic she kept there.

"Kill him, Redwood," Jade ordered, getting into the back seat of the limo.

Cris dove to the side as Jill Washington and Redwood both fired. Redwood missed by inches. Jill didn't.

Her bullet creased Redwood's side, making him stagger. His shirt's cornfield holo-projection rippled and died. He fired once more, then he bolted for the limo.

Jill fired again and hit him in the shoulder. He dove into the limo, which took off with a squeal of tires and a cloud of black exhaust.

Cristopher grabbed the pistol he'd dropped. Although he knew it was futile, he ran after the car. The GANs reached the end of Magee and turned right onto a major highway. They accelerated rapidly. In moments the limo vanished from sight.

Cris trotted back to rejoin Jill. The exertion made his head spin.

He found Jill leaning against the door of the heejee. Redwood's second shot had hit her leg. She pressed a piece of gauze from her heejee's first aid kit to the wound.

"Are you ok?" he asked. He took surgical tape from the kit and taped down the gauze.

"A scratch."

"Get in." He gestured at the co-pilot's seat. "I'll take her up."

"What about you?" she asked, noting his head. He pushed blood-clotted hair away from his eyes and took several deep breaths. His anger kept him going.

"I'll manage."

When she moved over, he got into the pilot's seat. The Beaumont heejee still had a half a tank of fuel left.

A police siren wailed in the air above them. Cris looked up and saw a police helijet with flashing blue lights circle down over the big Vonn-Grendel vehicle. They had apparently come to pick him up for his traffic violations.

He slipped on the headset and radioed control. "This is Beaumont Industries Flight—" he glanced at Jill.

"GBI-One."

"Flight GBI-One," he repeated. "We have priority A-One-Zero."

"GBI-One," replied Philadelphia Control. "You're cleared for takeoff. Priority A-One-Zero confirmed."

Idiots, thought Cris.

Traffic Control had to be the most inefficient government organization since the Post Office. This time they were even more fouled up than usual.

As the B.I. heejee lifted, the police ignored it completely.

Cris tried following the highway—the computer's map identified it as Roosevelt Boulevard—looking for the limousine. But with all the side roads, overhanging trees, and underpasses, it quickly became obvious he'd not be able to find them. They might even have pulled into a nearby garage.

"I don't suppose you know where they went," he said.

Jill shook her head glumly. "Somewhere in Philadelphia. I don't think they'd go to the Green Age headquarters here."

"That would be too obvious."

She paused and bit her lip. "Cristopher, I'm so sorry about this. I didn't know what they were planning to do. I had no idea they were going to involve Marica in their plans."

"What do you mean?" he said, glancing at her. "How could you have known?"

She didn't meet his gaze.

"Jill—what is it?"

"A few weeks ago," she said, "Jade Moon contacted me. She offered me a lot of money to spy on Beaumont. She said the Green Agers wanted to make sure Beaumont really used Pacifica's technology for the good of all. She claimed he wasn't planning to produce enough kelp to stop the famine—just enough to sell at a handsome profit."

"I get it," he said grimly. "I thought the same thing myself. Only I was willing to wait and see, to give him the benefit of the doubt."

Jill pulled nervously on her braid. "It seemed like a good cause, and I thought it wouldn't do any harm to look around. She made it sound like I'd be looking in trash baskets, stuff like that. Beaumont isn't one of my favorite people, and Jade Moon knew that. Besides, my parents needed the money—they're going to lose their farm. Jade Moon knew that too."

Cris stared out the window at the Philadelphia streets. He'd given up hope of finding the limousine. He listened to Jill, trying to understand, not wanting to believe she'd actually helped kidnap Marica.

"But then we went to Pacifica, and Harrison murdered those people. I began to realize that the Green Age wasn't as respectable as Jade Moon led me to believe—some of those GAN terrorists are in the Green Age, and I think she's one."

"Why didn't you just quit?" Cris asked.

"I tried to give her back the money, but she'd videotaped me taking it. She blackmailed me into working for them."

"So you helped kidnap Marica," Cristopher said glumly.

"No." Jill touched his arm. "I didn't know anything about that. I'd promised to look for papers about Pacifica, but I didn't find any. I didn't even send my parents the money."

"But what about the kidnapping?"

She shuddered. "Jade Moon arranged to meet me before the wedding. I was waiting for her when you arrived. Then her buddy Redwood showed up with a gun. He told me to wait in the heejee and be ready to take off. He didn't tell me why. Pretty soon Jade Moon and that other guy appeared with Marica in tow. Believe me," she pleaded, "if I had known what they were planning, I would've told Beaumont everything, even if it meant losing my job."

Cris shook his head. "You didn't do much when you did find out."

"What could I do with guns at our heads? I did the best I could. I saw you come after them. Redwood told me to take off or he'd kill me. I thought that other big guy might shoot you, so as we took off I bumped him with the heejee."

Cris remembered the way the heejee had knocked Forrest flat. He'd thought it was an accident at the time, but Jill could've done it deliberately.

"Redwood watched me the whole trip," she continued. "I couldn't get my gun out from under the dash until we landed."

"But why did you try to lose me when I followed you? Why didn't you go to autopilot?"

"Redwood knew something about heejees. I think he'd had some pilot training—maybe he dropped out. They wanted him along to watch me. Even though he probably couldn't pilot our heejee himself, he knew all about traffic control."

"Ah," said Cris. It all made a horrible amount of sense.

Jill looked out the window. "We're never going to find them. Why aren't you radioing the police?"

"I tried it. They don't believe the kidnapping took place. Beaumont denied it."

"But that doesn't make sense."

"Don't I know it," said Cris. "Maybe they contacted A.J. and told him not to talk to the police. He must have some reason."

"I suppose so." Jill rubbed her leg and looked away. "Beaumont must be sick with worry by now."

"We'll have to ask him," said Cris dejectedly, still studying the traffic below. "We're never going to find them now." There was nothing he could do except return to the *Lady Pecunia* to find out why Beaumont hadn't reported the kidnapping.

He punched in a course for New York and surrendered control to the autopilot. The dull ache in his stomach refused to go away. His head pounded. He had a lump in his throat that no amount of swallowing could get rid of.

I should have been there. I should have saved her.

He also felt disappointed in Jill. She'd tried to rationalize what she'd done by saying she'd been forced into it, but she'd accepted the Green Age's bribe. Maybe she wasn't as guilty as the rest, but she certainly deserved a share of the blame.

Or maybe there was something wrong with him, he thought. He always expected the best from people. Yet they rarely lived up to his expectations. When he was younger, people called him an idealist; behind his back they called him a fool. The older he got, the more he thought that was true.

"I'm really sorry," Jill said softly.

"I am too."

They spent the rest of the trip in silence, each reliving the past few hours, each wondering what they could have done differently to change the outcome, each feeling guilty.

FOURTEEN

THE *LADY PECUNIA* looked surprisingly deserted, thought Jill, as they reached the yacht. While she expected the guests would have departed, she also expected that police vehicles would have arrived.

She typed in the Beaumont access codes, allowing them to land on the yacht without triggering its auto-defenses.

Cris didn't bother with City Control; he simply landed. She guessed he was too fed up by now to bother with their red tape.

Control didn't seem to notice the heejee's disappearance from radar either. Jill didn't know whether that was due to their A-One-Zero priority or to Control's overworked and understaffed incompetence. She felt too exhausted and numb from all that had happened to care.

From the moment Jade Moon first asked her to spy on Beaumont, she'd been trapped in a web which closed more and more tightly around her. Now all she could do was wait for the spider to pounce.

She glanced at Cristopher, feeling more guilty than ever. She thought she'd found a friend in him. Now he'd caught the worst of it, and she couldn't begin to think how he felt. His face remained unreadable.

What do I expect? she thought. *This mess is partly my fault, and he almost got killed.*

"There's one thing I want you to understand," she said abruptly, breaking the silence between them as the heejee settled onto the helipad. "I don't have any excuses for what I did, but I wouldn't have gotten involved with Jade Moon in the first place if I hadn't thought that the Green Age's basic motives were good ones. I never realized how far they'd go."

"I'm more concerned about Marica than your lapses in judgment," said Cris.

He unstrapped himself, climbed out, and headed down toward the yacht's main deck with Jill trailing uneasily behind him.

"Hey, who are you?" called a security guard as they reached the bottom of the steps. Jill knew him vaguely: Bob Andrews, another of Beaumont's faceless minions.

"I'm Cristopher Morrisey. Where's Beaumont?"

Then Andrews caught sight of Jill. "Washington, what are you doing here? I heard you got kidnapped with Miss Vonn-Grendel."

"It's a long story," Cris answered for her. "We need to see Beaumont. We have important information about Marica Vonn-Grendel."

Andrews led them by the ship's bow, where empty banquet tables stood as bleak reminders of the day's events. The twilight's purple-gray sky looked oppressive, promising more rain soon.

Bypassing the main ballroom, still set with rows of chairs, they passed a smaller salon where stacks of wedding presents reached from floor to ceiling. Then they took the nearest elevator down a deck.

Andrews escorted them toward the small salon that served as Beaumont's personal den. Another bodyguard, Tony Giacco, stood watch outside. Giacco was a big bull of a man, with a face as beefy as his biceps. He looked as stiff as a mannequin until he saw visitors. Then he came to life, turning toward them and pulling his gun. When he recognized Jill and Cris, he relaxed a bit.

"It's okay," said Andrews. "These folks need to see Mr. Beaumont right away."

He knocked once on the door to the cabin. But before anyone could reply, Cris pushed it open and stormed in. Jill and the guards hurried after him.

Meticulously decorated, the room contained black leather couches, oriental screens, lacquered tables, and Chinese watercolors. A.J. sat behind a large ebony desk, drumming his fingers on a glass top covering inlaid ivory, pearl, and jade. It pictured a typical oriental scene of a pagoda, kimono-clad maidens, and coolie-hatted men. It matched the pictures on screens, bar, and other furniture in the room.

Only the plain white cabinet in the far corner appeared out of place. It contained fire extinguisher, first aid kit, and life belts. Beaumont, Jill knew, was a stickler for safety precautions.

Across from Beaumont sat a gray-haired man in a dark business suit. Jill recognized him: Lucas Ellsberg, Beaumont's top lawyer.

Jill had expected A.J. to look haggard and upset. Instead he seemed unaffected by the events of the last few hours. He still wore his black tuxedo. His blond hair was still neatly combed, his cowlick still slick and flat against his forehead. The only thing out-of-place was his bow tie, now loose and flapping around his unbuttoned collar.

When they burst into the room, he looked startled. His stare fastened on Jill.

"What are you doing here? You're supposed—" He stopped in mid-sentence, looking back and forth between the two of them. Then he said somewhat cautiously, "I thought you'd been kidnapped, too."

Jill wouldn't meet his gaze. She edged back toward the door, unsure how to explain her role in the kidnapping, and not wanting to try.

Beaumont got to his feet and leaned heavily on the desktop. "What happened to Marica?"

Cris quickly sketched out the kidnapping and his aborted rescue attempt in Philadelphia. Strangely, Jill thought, he said nothing about her taking the bribe.

When Cris finished, he paused for a moment. Then his voice took on an accusatory tone. "Why didn't you call the police?"

Beaumont pointed to a piece of paper in front of him. "They sent me a note warning me not to, or they'd kill Marica."

"And you listened to it?" Cris glared. "You should've contacted them anyway. If you had, they would've caught up with the kidnappers when they landed the heejee."

"Perhaps you'd better take a look at this note—it's pretty clear that if the police interfere in any way, Marica's going to die. They've set the swap for the center of Grand Central Station, where they'll be able to monitor our moves pretty effectively. If they even *suspect* police are involved, they'll kill Marica. After what you've said about them, I don't think Jade Moon and the others are just Green Agers—they're terrorists in the Green Action Now! movement. I know from experience that GANs *will* do what they threaten if you push them. They blew up one of my office buildings when I wouldn't shut down a nuclear power plant in Georgia."

Cris picked up the note and quickly scanned it. It gave long and precise instructions on where and when to meet and what to bring. They wanted the DNA signature of Beaumont's special bacteria.

When Cris finished, he looked at Jill, startled and scared. "They're going to wire her with *explosives*," he said. "If A.J. doesn't give them the Pacifica data at eight o'clock tomorrow night, they're going to blow her up."

"No," Jill breathed, aghast.

Cris looked at Beaumont. "We've got to stop them!"

Beaumont's face grew hard. "I'm taking care of it."

Cris stared at him coldly. "What happened to that man named Forrest who fell off the yacht during the kidnapping— did you pick him up? Maybe you can get information from him on where they took Marica."

"Unfortunately, he's dead. One of my guards shot him." Beaumont turned to Jill. "What about you, Washington? Why did you fly that heejee?"

Jill shifted uncomfortably. She didn't know how to explain her part in this to him. It had been easier to talk to Cris. Cris had at least partially understand what she'd done, even if he couldn't forgive her. But Beaumont would never understand. She'd betrayed him; that was all he'd think about.

Steeling herself, she knew she'd have to face him eventually. She might as well get it over with. "I'm sorry, sir, I shouldn't have trusted Jade Moon—"

"They forced Jill to fly the heejee," interrupted Cris. "They held a gun on her. There was nothing she could do."

Jill glanced at him in astonishment. He hated what she'd done, yet he was protecting her. She felt more ashamed than ever. She knew she should tell Beaumont the truth, but somehow she couldn't make herself speak.

"But why take Marica *now*?" Cristopher continued, shaking his head. "I just don't understand."

Beaumont glanced at the guards. "You can go," he said, gesturing toward the door. Andrews nodded and left. Giacco followed, closing the door behind them.

Cris said, "Why have the GANs kidnapped Marica? You're going to use Pacifica to stop the famines. All the radical environmental groups should be flocking to support you."

"I don't know, but they've demanded I give them my Pacifica plans."

"Can you deliver it to them?"

Beaumont pointed to a beautiful Degas painting of ballerinas at a practice bar. It hung behind his desk. "All the information's in my safe—the sum total of Pacifica's design on a master set of computer disks. I always travel with them in case I need to refer to them. Jade Moon obviously learned a lot about my operation from Marica."

"I still think you should call the police," Cris said.

"I'm surprised, Morrisey. For all your fawning over Marica, how can you even *think* of risking her life like that? Don't you care what happens to her? I'm going to follow the note's instructions to the letter, and that means no police. I've already got private detectives and my security teams working on it. If they find Marica before the deadline, fine. If not, I'll pay the ransom."

Cris shook his head stubbornly. "There's no guarantee that they'll release Marica. We already know some of the people involved. The police have experience with situations like this. Give them a chance!"

"I've already made my decision."

"And what if your decision's wrong?" Cris argued. "It's Marica's life we're talking about!"

"I knew you'd be trouble the moment I heard you got mixed up in this. Didn't I tell you, Lucas?" Beaumont looked at his lawyer.

Cris stalked to the desk and glared across at Beaumont. "I want some assurance that everything goes smoothly paying the ransom. At least let me help. There must be something I can do . . ."

"All right," said Beaumont. "As long as you're here, I guess you ought to be in on this every step of the way. Don't you think so, Lucas?"

The lawyer looked as though someone had just poured maple syrup all over his spaghetti dinner.

"Oh, er, sure."

"Everyone knows how fond Morrisey is of his ex-wife. It will be fitting if he helps us." Beaumont sat down and leaned back in his swivel chair. "Lucas and I were discussing what's the best way to handle this ransom thing. I think you'll be an excellent witness to what happens. I want you to be with us the whole way."

"All right. I want to make sure everything goes according to plan," said Cris.

"Good. That's settled, then."

"How did you keep the kidnapping quiet? Some of the guests must have heard the shots."

"I told them gate-crashers were acting up. I explained that the party had to end early due to security problems. That's far more believable than wild tales of kidnapping."

"I guess so," said Cris.

"I think it's best if you spend the night here, in case any news comes in. I'll let you know if my detectives turn up anything."

Beaumont walked over to the door and called in Giacco. "Tony, take Mr. Morrisey down to cabin 19. He'll be staying the night."

"Sure thing, Mr. Beaumont, I'll escort him down there."

Cris took a long look at the muscular guard, hesitated for a moment, and then glanced at Jill. "I'll see you in the morning."

"Good night," she said.

As the door closed behind them, the lawyer, Lucas Ellsberg, hunched forward in his chair. "Is that such a good idea?" he asked.

"Don't worry, it'll all be over in another day," Beaumont replied. "I don't want him messing anything else up. He'll be an excellent witness that I'm doing all I can to help get Marica back. I think I'll have him talk to the detectives tomorrow."

A.J. turned to Jill. "You've had a rough day. Why don't you get some sleep? Go on, don't worry. We're going to get Marica back." He pointed firmly at the door.

Reluctantly, Jill left. Something wasn't quite right, but she couldn't put her finger on it. She hesitated outside the stateroom. There were no guards anywhere in sight.

What was wrong with Beaumont? she asked herself. He'd hardly questioned them at all about what had happened. And really, Cristopher was right, why not bring in the police? They might be able to trace the kidnappers.

As she leaned back against the stateroom door, trying to

figure out what she should do, she realized that it hadn't latched behind her. It opened a crack. She could hear Beaumont and Ellsberg arguing inside.

"Why do you want Morrisey in on this?" said Ellsberg.

"He's a troublemaker. The best way to control him is to keep him where we can see what he's doing. I don't want him running off to the police on a whim."

Quietly, Jill peered through the slightly open door.

"Actually, when he first walked into the room tonight, I thought the wisest move would be simply to kill him," said Beaumont.

Ellsberg's eyes widened, but he nodded grimly as though he'd heard Beaumont give such instructions before.

"Then I thought better of it. Morrisey is the perfect witness to the fact that I tried to pay the ransom. He'll never realize I'm merely going through the motions, giving those damn environmentalists useless data. There is no way in hell I'm going to give that half-assed GAN group or anyone else that bacteria. That kelp process is worth a fortune."

Beaumont's voice grew wistful. "It is too bad about Marica, it really it is. She's a beautiful woman . . . and very good in bed. But now that I have her shipping companies, that's all I really wanted. If the kidnappers kill her, well that is unfortunate. But I won't ruin this Pacifica deal for her sake."

Jill stood frozen against the door with her body pressed tightly against the finger-wide crack.

"Under the terms of your prenuptial agreement, if Marica dies you'll inherit everything, her whole shipping empire," said the lawyer.

"Yes, I know. Too bad about Marica, isn't it?" Beaumont said slowly.

"But Morrisey could raise a stink about the way you've handled this kidnapping."

"It's a shame the kidnappers didn't kill him," mused Beaumont. "But don't worry, I'm going to use him to my advantage. He'll be the perfect witness that everything is on the up and up. He'll see me get ready to pay these Green Agers what they demand. He'll be convinced I did everything to save my pretty young bride, and he'll tell the world about it. He'll never realize I substituted phony stuff for the ransom. And if Jade Moon ends up killing Marica, well, it will be unfortunate, but not all *that* unfortunate for me."

Then the forward elevator opened and one of A.J.'s bodyguards appeared. Jill gently let the stateroom door close behind her and, trying to hide her confusion over what she'd heard, smiled at Tony Giacco. He gave her a nod as he sauntered up and resumed his post outside Beaumont's den.

"Did Mr. Morrisey get to his quarters okay?" she asked, trying to seem casual.

"Yeah," he smiled at her shyly. His head looked too small for his overdeveloped body.

"I'd better get along to my room. I've had a very hectic day."

"Yeah. Hope to see you later," he said.

Jill took the aft elevator down to the crew deck and went to her small cabin. It was about the same size as a pullman car, merely wide enough for a bunk bed, with a tiny washroom and closet at the back. A first aid kit and life jacket hung on the wall like odd decorations.

She immediately opened the porthole; the tang of salt air and pollution began to seep in. Still, it was better than nothing; the small cabin made her faintly claustrophobic. Although they were docked, she thought she could feel the boat sway slightly, up and down, left then right. She longed to be anywhere else.

What am I supposed to do now? she wondered. She'd really gotten herself into a mess. She felt partially responsible for Marica's kidnapping, and now it looked as though Beaumont didn't intend to pay the ransom. She hadn't thought much of him before, but he was a worse bastard than she'd imagined.

She stared out across the dark water, thinking of Pacifica. The sea's power could be such a help to the world, with Beaumont Industries' new technology to tap it. The kelp farms could stop famine and perhaps help reverse the Greenhouse Effect. But Jade Moon was undoubtedly right, Beaumont had never intended to share his technology in the first place. He'd sacrifice his wife's life to keep it and the power it brought him. The man had to be stopped.

It would be so simple to forget what she'd heard. She lay down on the bunk bed and shut her eyes, trying to squeeze out her memories. She wished she were back in Missouri, on the farm she remembered from her childhood—verdant hillsides, magical brooks that always led to new adventures no matter how many times you'd been there before, wide fields of corn where you could lose yourself forever.

But she couldn't easily forget what had happened. She felt compelled to do something to help Marica. She didn't fully know why—perhaps to ease her conscience, perhaps because of her friendship with Cris, perhaps even because of her parents and the Baptist do-good view of life they'd tried to instill in her. She couldn't just sit back and do nothing.

She sat up slowly, unsure of her resolve. It would be devastating for her family if she lost this job, if she ended up in jail. But if she didn't do anything, Marica might end up dead.

Finally she picked up the phone and dialed inter-ship to the maintenance department. Her stomach knotted. She felt as though she'd been swallowing rocks.

"Hi, this is Jill Washington," she said in her usual get-down-to-business voice. "Mr. Beaumont may be using the heejee tonight. Please have it checked out and refueled. Make it snappy."

She wasn't quite sure what to do next, but she had to be ready for anything.

She opened her purse and pulled out her company-issued gun. She checked the clip—almost empty. She rummaged through the cabinet above her bunk until she found the package of spare clips, replaced the one in the gun, and put several more into her purse.

She had to make up for the harm she'd done in listening to Jade Moon in the first place. She wanted to feel clean again

FIFTEEN

MARICA FELT like hell. Her best friend had betrayed her, and now she was a hostage, as helpless to escape or fight back as she'd been as a child. It *hurt*, and that made her angry.

She paced the length of her prison, stopping every few minutes to kick or hit the door leading to the hall. It didn't do any good. Deep inside she'd already realized the door was too strong, and only her stubborn pride kept her at it. They weren't going to let her out. And, in this old, abandoned apartment building, nobody but the GANs would ever hear her.

Her tongue flicked against the corners of her mouth. The gag had cut into her lips, and now they burned almost as much as the raw patches on her wrists where she'd struggled against her bonds. She thought she tasted blood.

I've got to get out of here.

For what seemed like the hundredth time, she took a survey of her prison, looking for any escape route or weapon. Nothing suggested itself. Solidly cemented bricks filled the both windows. A lone 40-watt light bulb dangled from a thin wire, casting a jaundiced glow over faded, peeling floral print wallpaper. The oak-plank floor had been swept clean recently; she couldn't see any dust. The too-solid oak door completed the room.

The GANs had left her a filthy blanket. She'd spread it out in the back corner, next to the bathroom's door.

She wandered into the bathroom, looking everywhere, finding nothing of use. It didn't have its own light anymore; the electrical fixtures, along with the sink and medicine cabinet, had all been ripped out, leaving gaping holes in the plaster. She could barely make out the graffiti, which proclaimed crude slogans in giant spray-painted letters across one wall.

The toilet seat had been ripped off. A tar-black residue encrusted the bare bowl beneath. Although the tank bent away from the wall, amazingly it still flushed, which was about the only thing Marica had to be thankful for in the last eight hours.

A jut of pipe where the sink had been slowly leaked water. Drops splashed to the floor, spreading an unhealthy looking mildew stain across tiles too chipped and dirty for her to guess their original color.

Marica touched the pipe and let a few drops of water trickle onto her fingers. Gently, she wet the abrasions around her mouth.

She prayed they wouldn't decide to tie her up again. They had kept her gagged and bound for the entire trip from New York to Philadelphia. They'd been planning to take her to some sort of 'safe house' there. But when Cristopher showed up unexpectedly, Jade Moon had suddenly changed plans, fearing he might be able to track them. So instead of waiting until morning, they'd stuffed Marica into the back of an automobile and driven her back to New York.

She'd felt as though she were going to die, crammed into that tight, suffocating space, not knowing where they were going or what was going to happen to her. Every sound seemed amplified, every movement of the car more intense. The darkness pressed in, almost becoming a physical presence—weighing against her chest like a granite slab, smelling of burning rubber, tasting like bile.

She'd sunk into a whimpering state of self-pity for a long while, blaming herself for everything. *I wanted to believe in Jade,* she told herself. *I should have known better.*

Feeling afraid and helpless, she could have been twelve years old again—hiding in the back of her closet, knowing her father would be coming to find her, knowing he would soon begin touching her and hurting her . . . knowing that there was nothing she could do.

She'd believed that it was all her fault. Nothing she did came out right. Didn't mommy and daddy tell her that often enough?

Other girls were prettier, brighter, slimmer, and had more personality. She was a mistake they'd made and now had to bear. The things they said ran through her mind like a river of sewage, poisoning, suffocating, burying her like the darkness inside the car's trunk.

Filled with despair, her mind sunk into a well of fear and self-hatred. Although it seemed impossible for her to feel any more empty or alone, her depression kept increasing. It drained her will, letting her accept anything that happened without protest.

Then the car hit a bump in the road. She was thrown forward and hit her head on the spare tire. And suddenly her self-pity evaporated as she found herself cursing the driver, the road, the Green Age, and Jade Moon—everyone and everything that had ever hurt her. The fury rose like a brushfire inside her, consuming everything in its path. It made her strong. Like a hot wind, it buoyed her upward toward the light.

In the past Marica had found anger an unexpected ally. She'd used it against loneliness and pain and despair. She used it now, and it made her strong.

I am a survivor. I will survive this, too.

Her anger renewed by the memory, she began to pace her prison again, studying the high ceilings, pounding at the door, screaming for her freedom.

Nobody came. Hours must have passed. Finally, exhausted, her hands aching, she sank down on her dirty rag of a blanket. There was nothing else to do but wait.

She thought of Cristopher and his courage in trying to rescue her. And just as suddenly she thought of how he'd beaten Harrison to a pulp on Rolugo. It seemed strange that a man so generous and loving, so sensitive and tender, could be driven to such extremes of violence.

A tear began to thread its way down her cheek. God, she wanted him here with her. *Cris . . .*

Throughout her life she'd felt alone, so terribly unwanted. She'd become all twisted up inside, she saw now. He was the only one who'd ever made her feel truly loved, who'd accepted her without question or blame, even when she hurt him. Sometimes she'd thought his love would change her. Perhaps that's why she'd run away from it.

Nervous energy wouldn't let her sit. She stood and prowled the bathroom once more. The pipes were solidly attached to the walls. The electrical sockets gaped emptily. There was no mirror. There was nothing she could remove from the cabinet's empty hole. Cement and bricks sealed the bathroom window.

She used the toilet and flushed it. The water gurgled up slowly, filling the bowl.

The flush —

The thought startled her. She pulled the lid off the tank. Sure enough, a metal rod connected the handle to a clap valve.

The rest of the mechanism was made of lightweight plastic or too small to be useful, but the rod would make a weapon of sorts. It wouldn't bend, and the pointed end could do some real damage if it caught an eye.

"Yes!" she breathed, jabbing at the wall with it.

As she noticed the bricked-up window, an idea hit. She began to hone one end of the rod against the cement. Slowly the metal began to sharpen.

She imagined stabbing Jade Moon. She pictured the rod plunging into Jade's skin, crimson blood running down the false emerald face. For an instant her whole body tingled with excitement, as though she'd really had the courage to strike back.

Then her stomach winched another notch tighter. *It's just a dream,* she told herself, *as fake as Jade's friendship.* She'd probably never have the courage, let alone the opportunity. *But if I did . . . I'd kill her, I know it.*

She'd seen beneath Jade's face-paint on several occasions: such pale, almost porcelain-white skin, she'd thought at the time. The epicanthic folds at the corners of Jade's eyes reflected her mother's Chinese origins, which was one reason Jade had chosen an oriental-sounding name when she'd become a member of the Green Age. But the rest of her features were from a fine-boned English father.

Jade had never really explained why she chose to veil her features. Dyes, face paints, and removable tatoos were commonplace for special occasions, but few people, even among the glitterfolk, went to such extremes.

Now Marica thought she understood. There was a mask beneath the mask, a hidden person who hadn't wanted her true personality to show.

Jade had seemed so caring and loving. Always so sweet — thoughtfully giving Marica presents, always cheerfully dispensing advice, always dishing out praise.

About as sweet as a razor blade in a candied apple, Marica thought bitterly. The blade had revealed itself with startling swiftness. *As if kidnapping me weren't bad enough, she did it on my wedding day . . . no matter what her motives, that's unspeakable.*

As Marica brooded, she honed her little metal rod. It took hours, but finally it had a needle-sharp point. She jabbed it into the wall again and again, ripping faded wallpaper in jagged gashes. She wished it were Jade's throat.

At last she stopped out of sheer exhaustion and sank to the floor in the bathroom doorway. She felt cold and sick. Her arms began to tremble uncontrollably. She reached for her blanket and pulled it over her shoulders. It stank of urine and sweat, but its warmth somehow comforted.

Tears welled up in her eyes. She tried to fight it, but she began to sob uncontrollably.

Masquerade. She didn't know which was worse, Jade's or her own. She recreated herself every day. Was Jade's betrayal any worse than the countless times she'd hurt Cristopher? It struck her as ironic that someone who'd played so many mind-games had been betrayed by someone just as adept. And it struck her as hypocritical that she, of all people, could so soundly castigate Jade's duplicity.

She began to laugh and weep together. It would have been funnier if it hadn't been so very sad.

Gradually her sobs eased into little mewing whimpers, until she had no tears left. Shivering, she pulled the blanket tighter. She curled into a ball, clutching the thin metal rod like a knife.

She felt drained of emotion. All that remained was one clear thought which she could not doubt for a moment.

She really did love Cristopher.

She had survived many horrible things in her life and, she was going to survive this one, too. Somehow she was going to get back to him.

SIXTEEN

CRISTOPHER KICKED off his blanket and lay staring at the bunk above. He felt too hot and uncomfortable to sleep, even if he could have wiped his mind free from troubling memories.

The bodyguard had given him some spare clothes, including the slightly too-tight pajamas he now wore. *Probably Beaumont's clothes,* he thought with some disgust.

He fluffed up his pillow, wedged his hand under his head in the exact position he liked, and tried to force his mind to go blank. It was impossible. He couldn't help but think of Marica, lying bound and gagged somewhere, or locked in a suffocating closet, or even dead, her body abandoned in the brush on some remote wooded hillside. The fear knifed through him.

I have to get to sleep, he told himself. *I have to be fresh in the morning if I'm going to get anywhere.* But the harder he tried, the more sleep eluded him.

His thoughts returned to Marica, to the day they'd first met in the Museum of Modern Art. Everything had seemed perfect. They'd spent hours together, exploring the exhibits, sharing their love of artwork.

"I lose myself in these paintings," Marica had said. "They're like a whole world to me." The words hadn't meant much to him at the time, but now they took on whole new shades of meaning. He hadn't realized then the pain she'd been hiding.

Thinking back, he should have known something troubled her deeply. He remembered her reaction to a pair of Edward Munch lithographs on display. In one, 'The Scream,' a strange figure more like a fetus than a man had its mouth twisted open in a gaping 'O'—so wide it seemed a tunnel into his soul. Marica stared at it and said, "That's me."

She sneered at another, two silhouetted lovers in 'The Kiss.' Contemptuously she called it "another false depiction of love," and mentioned that "the only true love is self-love—you can't get hurt from that kind."

She was vulnerable during those first few hours the way she never was later on in their relationship. Perhaps she found it possible to open up to a stranger the way she never could to someone she knew. When he finally told her he was the artist who had done 'The Rose,' the hologram she'd been studying when they met, she became a different Marica—the laughing, coquettish, charming Marica who dazzled every man she met. The woman who wanted to make him another conquest. The Marica who'd found that by controlling men she could reclaim a tiny piece of the child still within her, the little girl who couldn't stop a father from raping her whenever he'd wanted.

She might have thought she'd healed from the terrible hurt, but it had festered deep inside. Probably without realizing it, she'd subjected every men who ever loved her to a perverse sort of revenge—she manipulated them before they could hurt her, she broke their hearts before they broke hers, she used them before they used her.

Now that she finally trusted him enough to tell him her secret, perhaps true healing would follow. He prayed that was true.

A sound broke the quiet. He sat up, wondering if he'd imagined it, straining to hear.

It came again—a soft tapping.

Cris rolled to his feet, crossed to the door, and flung it open. Jill Washington stood there.

"What's going on—" he began.

She glanced up and down the corridor as though afraid someone might have followed her, pushed into his cabin, then closed the door tightly. Cris switched on the overhead lights. Their sudden glare showed the tension in her face.

Jill whispered, "I overheard Beaumont talking to that lawyer of his, Ellsberg, when they thought I was out of earshot. They're not going to pay the ransom. Beaumont's just going through the motions—he's planning to give them fake data instead. Or maybe he'll arrive a little too late."

"What do you mean—not pay the ransom?" Cris demanded. "God, Jill, why would he do that? It would really put Marica in danger. These GANs aren't kidding around—A.J. should know that, after all the damage that Harrison did on Pacifica."

"I'm sorry to have to tell you this, but from what I overheard, Beaumont doesn't care *what* happens to Marica. He mentioned something about getting her shipping company, now that they are married. If she's dead, it all goes to him. It's tied in to Pacifica somehow."

Sinking back down on the edge of the bed, Cris struggled to sort out what Jill told him. Marica did own a large shipping company, one of the largest in the world. Of course Beaumont would want it—he needed ships to transport kelp and fish from Pacifica to the rest of the world.

"He doesn't want to give up the bacteria or the technology that Pacifica developed," Jill continued. "If the kidnappers release Marica, that's fine. But if they don't, he doesn't care. Under the terms of their prenuptial agreement, Beaumont gets her assets if Marica dies."

"But A.J. said he would release the Pacifica technology."

Jill shook her head. "He lied to us. I think he's planning on raising only enough kelp to make a vast profit, not enough to solve the world's food crisis. And as for the various alternate forms of energy they're using at Pacifica, they're merely for show. Beaumont's never going to produce them commercially—he owns too many oil fields and refineries, not to mention lucrative pollution-control companies. He's not going to risk his financial empire to introduce non-polluting energy sources."

"What am I going to do," Cris said, a wave of despair washing over him, "if Beaumont doesn't pay the ransom?" He felt drained of energy. "Beaumont has to pay them. I'll go to the police if he won't!" Now that he and Marica finally had a chance to make it together, he couldn't let anything happen to her.

"I've been thinking about it, Cris, and we can't risk that," Jill said. "They'll kill Marica if there's even a hint of police involvement. It doesn't matter whether the Green Age hierarchy or a handful of radical members arranged the kidnapping. The Church is going to cover up its involvement, no matter how small. And they're powerful enough to do it. If there's any publicity, Jade Moon and the others will go underground. Without a ransom, they might just as well kill Marica."

"I'll make him pay the ransom." Cris grabbed one of the shirts that Tony Giacco had given him and quickly dressed in one of Beaumont's old suits. He tucked the gun that had belonged to Forrest into the jacket pocket.

Jill looked discreetly at her feet, although Cris knew she'd already seen him wearing far less.

When he reached for the door, Jill put a hand reassuringly on his arm. Cris wondered if he were being fair to her. He hadn't had a chance to tell her that things had changed between Marica and himself. He didn't know how to bring up the subject. He felt as awkward as a schoolboy when it came to relationships.

"Jill," he began, "I want you to understand one thing about Marica. I—"

"You love her," Jill smoothed the shaggy lock of hair back from his eyes. "And you'll do anything you can to make sure she's safe. Hey, pal, I know. What happened between us was something special, but it came out of need more than love."

Cris smiled. "I guess you do understand. If Marica gets out of this, I'm going to do everything I can to get her back. We talked after the wedding. She said she loves me. I think we may be able to have a second chance together."

"I hope it works out the way you want. I just pray we can free her."

"I've got to see Beaumont, convince him to pay that ransom." He drew a deep breath and headed into the hallway.

Jill tagged after him. "How can you make Beaumont do anything he doesn't want to?"

Cris paused at the elevator door. "I'll threaten to go to the police and the press, to blow the lid off this thing."

"I don't know . . ." Jill opened her purse slightly and held it up for Cris to look inside. Her brightly polished semi-automatic lay inside. "Perhaps there are other ways to convince him."

"I don't think threatening him is going to do any good. As much as I dislike the man, I'm not going to shoot him. He's savvy enough to realize that."

"Well, I might," said Jill with a gritty little smile that made him almost believe her.

"You *wouldn't?*"

Then Jill signed, leaning back against the elevator wall. "No, I guess I wouldn't. But maybe he won't know that."

They walked slowly toward Beaumont's den. Tony Giacco still stood on watch outside.

Jill purposefully took the lead. "Hey, Tony," she said as they approached. "Is that lawyer still with Beaumont?"

"No, he just left."

"Oh, good. Hey, why don't you take a break while I stand watch. Mr. Morrisey needs to talk to Mr. Beaumont again. Jill had acted as one of Beaumont's bodyguards several times in the past, so there was nothing unusual about her offer.

"Hey, thanks, that's nice of you. I'd like to get off my feet for a few minutes."

As Tony headed aft, Jill knocked on the Beaumont's door, then opened it. She nodded to Cris. "Good luck."

"Thanks." He slipped in, leaving Jill on guard.

Beaumont still sat at his desk. A small computer now lay on top. He diligently typed something, oblivious to the world around him.

"All right, Beaumont," Cris said. "I think it is time for another little chat."

Beaumont bolted up in his chair at the unexpected intrusion. When he saw Cris, a worried frown creased his forehead.

"What now, Morrisey? I thought you were in your cabin."

"I want to know what's really going on."

"What do you mean?"

"You're not planning on paying Marica's ransom."

"I don't know what you're talking about."

Cris stalked over to the desk. "Jill Washington overheard what you were telling your lawyer. You're planning to give the Green Age fake information." He paused, sweat beginning to sheen his forehead. "You don't even care if Marica dies."

"I knew you were going to be trouble the minute I heard you'd gotten involved." Beaumont rolled backwards in his chair, studying Cristopher the way an exterminator might look at a termite. "You should mind your own business."

"Marica *is* my business."

"Your old business, Morrisey. She's *my* wife now."

"And apparently you don't care much about her. You'd rather lose her than risk your precious Pacifica deal!"

"I care. What I'm preparing would fool anybody—I'm working on the data right now." Beaumont gestured at the stack of computer disks in front of him. They were round CD Rom disks, about the size of pre-1970 Silver dollars. It seemed computers became smaller, yet more powerful every year. As a holo-artist Cristopher had become an expert with them. Sometimes it seemed as though he spent more time keeping up with the latest advances than in producing art.

He gave the CDR disks a contemptuous wave. "We can't take that chance. Harrison probably already fed the Green Age enough information about Pacifica so they'll be able to spot any discrepancies. They'll have an expert at the ransom drop to examine what you give them. Read that note—they mean business!"

Beaumont's blue eyes looked untroubled. "Trust me."

"God damn you—the note claims they're going to pack Marica up in a trunk full of plastic explosives and put her into a locker! If they get *one hint* that you aren't giving them what they want, they'll let it detonate instead of giving you the key. These GANs are crazy. Do you remember a few years ago when they wrecked that nuclear plant to make a point and almost caused a meltdown?"

Beaumont sighed. "Frankly, Morrisey, you're right. I don't really care what happens to Marica. But I *do* care about Pacifica. That project has cost me billions to set up, and the Vonn-Grendel shipping company is the last piece I need to make the whole plan operational. I've got that now, with or without Marica. I'm not giving away the plans for the whole setup to some environmental nuts who will pass them out to my competitors."

Cris stared, shocked. "You're a real scum. You'd let the whole world starve as long as you make a profit."

"Be realistic. You read the ransom note. The kidnappers want me *personally* delivering the ransom. I'll give them what I want to give them, and that's all there is to it. Nothing you can do will change my mind. Try to stop me and I won't give anything to the kidnappers, and Marica won't have any chance at all."

"I can't believe you're saying that," Cris said, watching Beaumont carefully.

"You're just infatuated with Marica. If you're smart, you'll find someone else . . . Jill Washington, maybe." He grinned. "I'll give you a million dollars, tax free, if you walk away right now." Beaumont started to stand, leaning halfway in and halfway out of his armchair.

"You bastard, you can't buy me! If you don't deliver the right information to Jade Moon, I'll go to the newsfeeds—and the police, too!"

"I should have killed you earlier this evening," Beaumont snarled, eyes suddenly cold and hard. As he spoke, he began reaching surreptitiously under his desk. "I think you've out-lived your usefulness."

Cris had almost been expecting such a move. As Beaumont pulled out a pistol, Cris dove across the desk. Cris hit his arm, hard. The gun spun away.

They began to struggle, Beaumont clawing at Cris's throat, Cris trying to pin Beaumont's arms.

"Giacco!" Beaumont shouted.

Cris glanced back to see Jill enter the room. She closed and locked the door.

Beaumont must have felt the gun in Cris's jacket. Thrusting his hand into Cris's pocket, he pulled it out. His finger fumbled for the trigger.

Seizing Beaumont's wrist, Cris threw all his weight forward in a desperate move. The armchair rolled backwards.

Losing his balance, Beaumont slid to the floor, Cris on top of him.

Cris kneed Beaumont in the stomach as hard as he could. A.J. turned green and began to gasp for air. Cris knocked the pistol away. Skittering across the plush carpet like a hockey puck, the gun slammed into the nearest Chinese screen.

Beaumont went limp, gasping. His eyes looked part angry, part sick, part frustrated.

Cristopher reared back and punched Beaumont in the face as hard as he could. Beaumont's eyes went glassy.

"Stop it!" Jill said. She picked up Cris's pistol from the floor and aimed it at Beaumont. "I'll cover him."

But Cris hadn't lost control of himself the way he had with Harrison. He forcibly held his anger in check, controlling his emotions. Roughly he pulled Beaumont's jacket back, tempo-rarily pinning his arms. Then he removed Beaumont's bow-tie and tied his hands with it.

Beaumont began to struggle feebly. Cris hit him again, and he lay still.

"Tony Giacco will be back any minute," said Jill. "What are we going to do?"

Cristopher glanced quickly around the room. "Try his desk—maybe there's some tape."

"Better yet, the first aid kit," Jill said. She ran to the corner cabinet and pulled it out from under a stack of life preservers.

Rummaging around inside, she pulled out a roll of medical tape. In a minute they had taped Beaumont's mouth so he couldn't yell for his bodyguard again, reinforced the bonds on his hands, and tied his feet together.

As they worked, Jill kept shaking her head. "But what do we do now?" she asked again. "Beaumont isn't just anyone—you can't tie him up and get away with it. And even if you could, how do we get off his yacht with guards everywhere?"

Cristopher sat back on his heels, trying to think of a way out. *And what about Marica?* he wondered. Beaumont was right—even if he took the computer disks to the Grand Central Station rendezvous, the kidnappers would never show themselves. They'd be looking for Beaumont. He didn't think he'd be able to force Beaumont to walk anywhere unwillingly, let alone into the middle of Grand Central.

"Cris?" Jill said.

"I know." He stood up and pounded his fist against the ebony desk. "We need Beaumont to get off the ship, and we need Beaumont to drop off the ransom." He glared down at the industrialist. "Damn it, Beaumont's too stubborn to do what we tell him too, even with a gun at his head!"

Beaumont's glare took on a smugly satisfied look.

"You'll never make him do what we want," Jill agreed. "He's not like your hologram."

"Hologram? That's it." Cris grabbed Jill's shoulders. "I gave them that holo I showed you as a wedding present. It's upstairs in that pile of gifts. I think I can change it into what we need, at least to get out of here." He rubbed his hands nervously. He felt unsure of himself and exhausted. Too much had happened. "And maybe it can be adapted into something to help Marica."

"Anything's worth a try."

"Let me have the gun," he said to Jill. "I'll keep an eye on Beaumont. See if you can find the holo and bring it back here. It's in a plain box, covered with white paper. It's cube-shaped and about two-feet square. I arrived pretty early, so it's probably on the bottom of the pile."

Suddenly someone knocked on the door.

"Don't worry," said Jill as she ran to answer it. "I'll find it."

Cristopher dragged Beaumont around behind the desk where he couldn't be seen, stuck the gun against his temple, and whispered "Don't even *think* about moving!"

He watched Jill open the door a crack. Tony Giacco stood there, a slightly confused look on his wide, bulldog face. She smiled sweetly at him.

"Hi, Tony, I'll be with you in a second. Mr. Beaumont wanted to talk to me, too."

She shut the door, and nodded reassuringly toward Cris. Then she silently mouthed a count of ten and opened the door just enough to slip out, keeping her body between Tony and the room as much as possible.

When the door closed, Cristopher settled into the desk's chair. He leaned forward and studied the mirror-thin computer screen. Beaumont had been copying files from one CDR disk to the other. From the highlighted files on the copy program, he could see how little information Beaumont actually selected for transfer to the bogus disk.

He glanced down at his prisoner. Beaumont had started squirming the minute Cris's attention had wavered.

"You're not going anywhere," Cris said, making his voice as hard and cold as he could. "And if you don't just lie there quietly, I'll knock you out."

Beaumont settled back, still glaring.

He's going to be trouble, Cris thought. I've got to tie him up better than that.

Opening the desk drawers, he rummaged through, looking for anything useful. Papers, business files, pens, routine office supplies—nothing interesting. Then he remembered the life jackets. Grinning, he fetched one from the corner cabinet. It didn't take long to put Beaumont's feet and arms through the holes and tie them in place. When he finished, A.J. was lying in a reverse fetal position, arms and legs curled behind his back. Now he couldn't even crawl.

Free to relax his attention from Beaumont, Cristopher went back to the computer. After five minutes of scanning through the bogus disk, he knew something was very, very wrong. The information was too obviously incomplete. Maybe A.J. had been planning to add more files, but Cris doubted it; the disk looked pretty much finished. The data would never pass even the most cursory of examinations, let alone the spot-verification the kidnappers had promised.

Cris copied all the information from the original disk onto the incomplete one. When he finished, he pocketed the original. Keeping an eye on Beaumont, he sorted through the other disks on the desk, quickly determining which were the originals and which had been altered. Then he copied the data until he had two complete sets of disks, keeping one for himself. As far as he could tell, they contained full technical specifications for the Pacifica project, including information on the development of the bacteria and its complete DNA sequence. It wouldn't be hard for another lab to engineer a copy now.

Next he checked Beaumont's safe. The Degas painting in front hung open. In the cavity behind he found a large amount of money, some jewelry, and some papers and CD Rom disks that related to Beaumont's many companies, but nothing more about Pacifica.

The ransom note lay on the big ebony desk next to the diskettes. Cris reread the instructions. They demanded that Beaumont himself deliver the Pacifica information, probably as extra insurance that no police would be involved. After all, Beaumont wouldn't want to be caught in any crossfire.

According to the note, Beaumont had to meet Jade Moon tomorrow night at eight. Cris wondered why the GANs hadn't kidnapped Beaumont himself. Although Beaumont Industries' security made A.J. a difficult target, he wasn't an impossible one, especially since the Green Agers had Jade Moon, Marica's reputed best friend, as an agent. But Beaumont was tough enough that he probably wouldn't have responded to physical threats. Besides, if he'd been kidnapped, who would've had the authority to trade Pacifica information for his release? No, the GANs had chosen their target well. They'd just erroneously assumed that Beaumont would do anything to rescue his new bride.

A loud knock interrupted his speculations. As he darted toward the door, he heard Jill on the other side: "Mr. Beaumont, I've brought that package you wanted."

Cris opened the door. Jill stood there, carrying the present, while Tony Giacco hovered behind her left shoulder.

"Sure. Mr. Beaumont's eager to see it," Cris replied.

He smiled politely over Jill's shoulder at the bodyguard, but his nervousness turned it into more of a grimace.

Jill entered, slamming the door shut behind her, just as a dull thudding began in the back of the room.

"What's that?" she demanded.

They ran to the desk and found Beaumont kicking awkwardly at the chair. Cris pulled him away, and Jill rolled him over so he couldn't do it again.

"Do you think Giacco heard that?" Cris asked.

"I don't think so," said Jill. "Here's the box."

She knelt over to Beaumont and checked his bonds. "He looks okay, except for his face—it's awfully red."

"It's going to get redder when he sees this."

Cristopher opened the package, revealing a clear square plastic box about a foot and a half on a side. An electrical cord running from the button had a switch near the plug. Inside you could see a layer of miniature lasers, circuit boards, and a tiny computer. Cris opened the box and began pulling out various components, which he stacked on the desk.

"You know," Cris said, holding up a CD Rom, "I can make this hologram say anything I want it to. Once I sampled Beaumont's voice and digitized it, I got an exact replica of its wave structure. It couldn't fool an expert, but it's enough like him to fool almost everyone else. Even his closest associates wouldn't be able to tell the difference."

With her eyes still on Beaumont, Jill asked, "How's that going to get us off the yacht? Maybe you were right the first time . . . maybe we ought to call the police, or the newspapers, or *something.*"

"The police aren't going to be much help," said Cris, as he began loading the software from the hologram-box onto Beaumont's computer. "You already said as much yourself. Besides, Beaumont owns Mayor Pollack. I don't want to call in anyone until Marica is safe. I haven't thought it all the way out, but I think we can make the ransom drop ourselves. Those computer disks on the desk hold all the information the kidnappers asked for—at least, I think they do."

"But what about Beaumont? Do you think we ought to dump him overboard or something?" She seemed uneasy at that prospect.

Cris laughed. "No. We'll keep him on ice until the ransom's paid. Then we'll go to the press and tell them what he tried to do. When the world finds out that he can stop the famine, but didn't want to, there'll be a huge scandal."

"I still don't see how we get out of here."

"Hold on a few more minutes, and I'll show you." He continued typing into the computer, changing various settings. On the flat screen, a tiny full-color image of A.J. Beaumont shifted as Cris manipulated its parameters. He planned to turn it into a full-size holographic projection. He could change the holo's movement and automatically synchronize the lips to any new words he encoded. It would be a lot of work, but he knew he could do it.

*   *   *

It took more than an hour before he was ready for the first test. Fortunately Tony Giacco, ever the obedient robot, never checked to see what was going on in his boss's office. Whenever the phone rang, which happened several times, Jill answered as though she were Beaumont's secretary, saying he would call back later.

Finishing the holo's final touches, Cris put the holo-box on the floor and said, "How's this?" as he pressed a button.

A full-size, three-dimensional image formed around the box: A.J. Beaumont, smiling and jovial, looking like he owned the world. The holo-Beaumont no longer made a transformation, but remained stable, looking indistinguishable from the real man . . . unless you tried to touch him.

The holo turned toward the cabin door and said, "Tony, I want you to go off-duty. Jill will act as my bodyguard for the moment. I'll be leaving the yacht tonight and be back here tomorrow. You are to be at the heejee pad tomorrow night at precisely ten-thirty p.m."

Jill smiled. "It sounds like him, but there's one problem— he's should be wearing a tux."

"Yeah. Let me see." Cristopher hunched over the keyboard, using the art programs on the CDR disk to alter the image. Most of the programs were tools he'd developed himself or altered from canned software. Fortunately colors and textures could be overlaid on images. For an artist of his caliber, turning a gray suit into a black tuxedo was a fairly routine task. He even added a bow-tie around the holo-Beaumont's neck. Someone standing a few inches away might notice that the tie wasn't quite right, but it would do. If he had a photograph of the real tux and tie, he could've made the image so real that not even Beaumont's tailor would have seen the difference up close.

He played the program again. The holo-Beaumont appeared before them, this time apparently wearing a tux almost identical to the one worn by the Beaumont on the floor.

Beaumont, seeing his double, began to thrash around again, trying to get free. Finally Cris had to threaten him. He subsided, glaring his hatred. *If looks could kill,* Cris thought.

He turned to Jill. "Is that good enough to get us by Tony Giacco?" he asked.

She shrugged. "I think so, but what if Tony says something, what about the reply?"

Cris unplugged the holo-box. The Beaumont image abruptly vanished. Then he took it behind the desk and did some more adjusting. He turned the image on and off until he obtained the illusion of Beaumont standing behind the desk. Cris took the holo-computer out of the box and hid it and the wiring behind Beaumont's own, slightly larger, computer.

"Get ready to ask him in," he instructed Jill.

She double-checked Beaumont, who was still firmly tied, and took a position by the door.

"Pretend you're Tony and talk to me."

He flipped a switch and the holo-Beaumont appeared.

Jill mimed opening the door and entering.

"Tony, I want you to go off-duty," said the holo, his lips perfectly in sync with the voice. "Jill will act as my bodyguard for the moment. I'll be leaving the yacht tonight and be back here tomorrow night. You'll be back on duty at ten p.m. tomorrow, precisely."

"Really, sir?" said Jill. "Who else will be going with you?"

There was a slight hesitation, and then the holo replied, "Mr. Morrisey will be accompanying me. Inform my staff in the morning that I won't be back until ten-thirty p.m."

"Yes, sir." Jill's mouth popped open in surprise.

"Ten-thirty p.m. precisely."

Jill returned to the desk. "How did you do it? It's just like Beaumont!"

"I've got the keyboard back here where I can type into it, and I've set it so that it will automatically synthesize my input into Beaumont's voice."

"It's great. I know Tony will go for it. But I don't see how you can use it to deliver the ransom tomorrow night. I don't mean to sound negative, but didn't you say the drop was in Grand Central Station?"

Cris nodded.

Jill walked over to the holo-Beaumont and poked her hand into his chest. It slid in without any resistance, as though the holo were an all-too-real-looking ghost.

"Take this into Grand Central and someone is bound to bump into it. If you could get that image to walk in somehow, the slightest touch would make the trick obvious."

"I know. But if we can get back to my studio, I think I can kludge up something that'll work. We're almost the same size . . . in fact, I'm wearing one of his suits. He loaned me some clothes."

They both glanced down at A.J. Although the tape masked the lower half of his face, there was no mistaking the rage twisting his normally cherubic face into something more troll-like. Becoming a prisoner had to be hard for Beaumont to bear, Cris knew. He'd be more frustrated at losing control of the situation than at being bound hand and foot.

"You're right," Jill had to admit. "I hadn't noticed it before, but you both have about the same build and coloring. But I still don't get it. Even if we have the Pacifica plans, the kidnappers won't show up unless they see Beaumont, and we can't have a hologram deliver them."

"I'm going to change the hologram," he said, winking at her. "You see, I'm going to become A.J. Beaumont."

SEVENTEEN

MARICA LAY in the semi-darkness of the bathroom, waiting. She'd been in a strange state of semi-awareness for most of the night, never quite sure if she'd actually fallen asleep or not, although she guessed she probably had. Her mind had been too filled with worries and memories. She shuddered. They were acid to her soul, eating away at her fragile ego and will to survive.

When are they going to come? she thought. As her fears had grown over the hours, so had her hunger. She had no way of knowing, but she guessed that almost a full day had passed since her abduction. A fast might be good for her figure, but it did nothing for her disposition. She'd rubbed her hand raw against the metal rod by nervously clenching and unclenching her fist.

She knew Jade wanted to swap her for Pacifica's plans, but she didn't know how or when the trade would take place. Since they hadn't bothered to feed her, she was beginning to wonder if they ever planned to let her go.

Further, Marica thought glumly, there seemed to her an equally good chance that A.J. would refuse to pay. She knew he was infatuated with her, but she wasn't naive enough to believe he really loved her. Still, she kept telling herself that he *would* pay, if not out of love, then out of self-preservation. The bad publicity if she died would be more devastating than the loss of any business secrets.

A noise in the hallway outside caught her attention. She climbed to her feet, pulling together the shreds of her resolve to fight, rather than be a victim again.

She held the metal rod behind the doorframe, where it couldn't be seen. One end of the blanket was clutched in her other hand, waiting to be tossed away or drawn up to hide her weapon, depending on who came in.

The door opened. Jade Moon entered, carrying a loaf of bread. The room's dim light made her painted skin look the color of pea-green vomit.

Jade halted just inside the bathroom. She was alone. Maybe she was vulnerable, thought Marica.

"Something for you to eat."

Jade Moon was still too far away. Marica realized that she should have been waiting right by the door.

"I don't feel well," she said. Pulling the blanket around so that its folds concealed the rod, she wobbled out into the main room, looking as though she were going to faint.

Jade's tone was brusque. "You're just hungry. Here, eat this, and you'll feel better." She put the loaf of bread on the floor.

By now Marica only stood a few feet away. Without warning, she whipped the blanket at Jade's eyes and released it. Lunging forward, she stabbed with the metal rod like a knife.

The thin shaft pierced Jade Moon's right shoulder.

As Jade screamed, Redwood and a second man ran into the room. They'd called him Meadowlark, which seemed an odd name for such a tall, reedy man with a gaunt face and badly discolored teeth.

Marica jabbed again and again at Jade, making several deep puncture wounds and cuts before Meadowlark grabbed her arm.

She kicked and fought as the two men pulled her away. Redwood awkwardly twisted the rod out of her hands. His left arm was in a sling due to the bullet wound he'd received when Cris had tried to rescue her. Then Meadowlark pinned and handcuffed her arms behind her back.

"Tie the bitch up," ordered Jade. She hunched over, clutching her shoulder in pain. Blood covered her fingers and soaked her dress.

"I'd better help you clean those wounds," said Meadowlark. "They look nasty. I thought you said she'd be easy as a pussycat to handle. Where the hell did she get this claw?" He studied the rod with a puzzled look. "I thought we'd cleaned all the debris out of this room; we must've missed something somewhere."

He brought in some rope and tied Marica hand and foot so that she could only move by crawling. Marica berated herself for having blown her one chance at escape.

Redwood picked up the loaf of bread and swung it teasingly above her head. "No food for you, Marica. You've been a bad girl."

Then the three left, slamming the door ominously behind

them. Marica felt a surge of terror. She'd been a fool to try anything. They were only going to make it worse for her now.

A few minutes later the door reopened, and Meadowlark wheeled in a large steamer-type trunk. It must have been more than 50 years old. He picked Marica up and put her in. Curled up, she just fit inside.

Meadowlark folded the dirty blanket and put it under her head for a pillow. Then he nervously ran his fingers through his dark, thinning hair.

"Don't worry," he said. "This will all be over in a couple of hours. With any luck your husband will give us what we want, and you'll be free."

"Should we put the bomb in now?" asked Redwood, coming into the room. He carried a briefcase with his good arm.

"Bomb?" cried Marica. She tried to pull her hands free of the cuffs, but they were too tight.

"It's not as bad as it sounds," Meadowlark said gently. He rechecked her ropes. "The exchange is taking place in Grand Central. We'll put this trunk in a locker. When your husband gives us the data we need, we'll check it and give him the key. He can easily switch off the device."

Marica shivered uncontrollably. "But why a bomb?"

"We need some easy way to kill you if Beaumont fails to show up or tries to trick us. It's a timer device, and we also have a remote transmitter in case of problems." He smiled, trying to comfort her. "But we're sure your husband will comply with our demands, Mrs. Beaumont. He loves you very much."

Marica wondered how Meadowlark could be so sure when she certainly wasn't. Had she misjudged A.J.? She hoped so.

"See if Jade wants us to give her the injection now," said Meadowlark.

"Okay," Redwood said, putting down the briefcase.

"What sort of an injection are you giving me?" Her voice shook.

"We're just going to knock you out for an hour or two so that you don't cause any trouble. We don't want you making any noise or causing a commotion, or conscious if we have to set the bomb goes off—we're not cruel. Don't worry, the injection won't hurt you."

Marica grimaced. *Not hurt me!* The man patted her head reassuringly, seemingly oblivious to the irony of his words.

Jade Moon came back into the room. She wore a new blouse that concealed most of the bandages on her shoulder. Smaller bandages hid the scratches on her arms.

"Get out," she said to Meadowlark. "I want to talk to Marica privately."

As soon as the door closed, Jade walked to the front of the trunk and looked down with a callous stare.

Marica felt a sudden chill inside. She found something menacing in Jade Moon now, an open hatred playing across that green face . . . hatred which had always been so carefully concealed in the past.

Then, with spiderlike grace, Jade Moon opened the briefcase and removed a small black box. "This is what's going to kill you," Jade said, as though she were ordering soup with dinner. She set it into the trunk, next to Marica's face. "It's a bomb— plastic explosives, timer, detonator. It will explode at eight-thirty, just a couple of hours from now."

Marica's throat tightened with fear. "You sound like you're going to kill me even if A.J. pays the ransom."

Jade laughed, and the sound grated like squeaky chalk. "He's not going to," she said confidently.

Marica tensed. "He's going to make Pacifica public soon anyway, so he'll give you the plans. Of course he will!"

"You don't understand, my dear friend Marica. Alex is not going to help the Green Agers . . . or anyone else. He's never going to make Pacifica's kelp-processing secrets public. I didn't plan to tell you all this, but after that little stunt you pulled . . ." Jade touched her bandaged shoulder. "I thought it would be better if your last thoughts were of how your dear husband and I will be together soon, comforting each other over your untimely death."

Marica's eyes widened.

"You see," Jade Moon said, "Pacifica is far too valuable to him—and *to me*. He wants you to die during this kidnapping. He planned the whole thing!"

"I don't understand."

"All along I've been working for Alex. I was with him when he conceived the plan months ago. You knew we were lovers once. Well, we *still are*."

Marica squirmed against the bonds, but there was no escape. "Why?" she whispered.

"Money, my dear. He needed your shipping companies to transport the processed kelp from Pacifica. With your record for month-long marriages, the only way he'd gain permanent control was if you died. He maneuvered you every step of the way. And I did my part as well."

Marica remembered all too well how Jade had encouraged her to meet A.J., telling her how charming he was, what a good catch, and even praising his prowess as a lover.

"Then none of you are Green Agers?"

Jade looked as though she wouldn't bother to answer anything further, but then changed her mind. She seemed to enjoy tormenting Marica with the truth.

"On the contrary," she said, "this whole thing is run by the terrorist arm of the Green Age, the GANs. I infiltrated on Alexander's orders. I helped plot activity against Beaumont competitors. I've been able to tell Alex about every plan the Green Age developed against him. Recently the GANs wanted me to recruit his pilot, Jill Washington, to spy on him. So I did. They never realized Beaumont knew about it, too, and made sure Jill never saw any valuable information.

"I was the one who convinced the GANs to kidnap you. I told them how much Alexander loves you. It's really quite funny. And all according to Alex's plan. He really has a brilliant mind." She gloated, relishing her sense of victory.

"The GANs think tonight's ransom drop is legitimate. But when Alex shows up, he'll give me obviously false information, which I'll show to Meadowlark and the others. Since they'll believe Beaumont is trying to double cross us, we'll just *have* to kill you. And the GANs will have no idea that Beaumont used them to commit murder. He'll be a grieving widower as far as the world is concerned."

Plots within plots, duplicity within duplicity. It would have been hard for Marica to accept if she hadn't been so used to her own brand of manipulation.

Jade Moon smiled smugly. "And what's so nice is the happy ending for Alexander and me. He'll get your ships and be rid of you. After we contact the media and tell them all about what the evil environmentalists did to him, we'll discredit the whole Green Age movement. Your death will be used to explain why Beaumont Industries must keep Pacifica a monopoly. You just can't trust anyone these days."

"And what do you get out of it?" Marica asked, her voice barely a whisper.

"After a little plastic surgery and a new name, I'll eventually become the new Mrs. Alexander James Beaumont."

Marica felt sick to her stomach. Jade's betrayal was bad enough, but A.J.'s was so much worse. He'd used her. Perhaps she deserved his cruelty; it seemed an ironic retribution for the way she'd tried to control him.

Jade looked inside the briefcase again and took out a needle and medicine bottle. Carefully, she prepared an injection of anesthetic.

"It's really too bad that you're going to miss the biggest headlines of your career. Little Miss Society Page, aren't you, with all your silly glitterfolk friends? I'll be so glad to be rid of them when this is done, you have no idea."

"A.J. is just going to use you, like he used me," said Marica, frantically trying to think of some way to change Jade's mind.

"He uses me and I use him, that's the way of things. I'll become Mrs. Beaumont, one of the richest and most powerful women in the world. And I'll know how to use that power, unlike you, darling, simpering little Marica."

Masks behind masks, thought Marica. Perhaps beneath all of Jade Moon's masks lay someone not that much different from Marica herself. She shuddered. Seeing herself as kindred to the merciless Jade Moon was the most shattering revelation of all. Marica had hidden behind protective deceptions for so long, she had become them. She felt ashamed, remembering the hurt she'd caused Cris so many times. Now she would never have the opportunity to make it up to him.

"Sweet dreams from your loving husband," smirked Jade, as she inserted the needle into Marica's arm.

EIGHTEEN

"IT'S FINISHED," said Cristopher.

Jill jerked awake with a start. She'd been nodding off again. *Have to watch that,* she thought.

Beaumont, hands and legs still tied, snored softly from the armchair. His head hung back at a steep angle and his mouth gaped open, showing perfect white teeth. He looked childlike and innocent. It was all an act, Jill knew, designed to make them feel guilty; Beaumont had played the role of victim to perfection during the long night and day since they'd removed him from his luxury yacht.

Fortunately kidnapping him had been easy. Giacco believed the hologram's orders absolutely. They'd lugged A.J. up to the heejee without being spotted and flown to Cris's apartment. In the darkness, it had been easy to carry him inside.

The difficult part had been all the work Cris needed to do on the hologram.

Cris stood in the doorway, turning right and left like a fashion model. He wore a safari-type vest covered with wires, memory wafers, amplifiers, power packs, and other components which had originally been part of the wedding present's holobox. But the vest didn't draw her eye the way his face did. Cris had put in blue contact lenses and shaved his head into a Marine Corps frizz.

Jill couldn't help but stare, thinking again how strange he looked—and how different. Without that shoulder length shaggy hair, Cris seemed a lot younger. Of course he'd only cut it to make the holo work properly, but it somehow suited him.

"Can you give me a hand?" he asked.

Jill rose and went over the wires and circuits with him. The voice amplifier against the skin of his neck was the trickiest part. If he whispered or spoke sub-vocally, the mike would pick up his input and feed it into the computer now spread out over the safari jacket, where it would be almost instantaneously converted into the digitized voice of A.J. Beaumont. She made sure the mike fitted firmly against his neck.

Cris put on his suit coat, concealing the computer-vest. "How does this look?"

It bulged very slightly under his arm. Jill pulled down on the vest and smoothed the layer of components until they no longer protruded noticeably.

"Fine," she said. "I really think this it's going to work!"

"We'll see."

Cris went back into his workroom and brought out a mask made from special holographic fabric. Sculpted to fit his head, it consisted of several layers of material, including nano-computer lattices for control, sensors, and elastic fiber-optic materials to transmit light and project images. Until activated, it looked more like a hockey mask than anything else.

Cris connected the disguise to the vest-computer and pulled it on. It completely covered his face and head; he peered out through eye-slots and breathed through small, round nostril holes.

"Can you breathe?" Jill asked.

He nodded. "It's bulky," he said, voice muffled, "and I can't see that well, but I think it'll do. The important thing is for it to work for the few minutes we need to make the drop."

He switched on the holo. Abruptly the mask shimmered; its blank surface became Beaumont's smiling face.

The illusion startled Jill. She hadn't expected it to work so well. Cris had been right: taking the extra time to rig up a more sophisticated projection device for just Beaumont's head had been worth it. They had discussed projecting Beaumont's whole image over someone smaller, like Jill, but it probably wouldn't have worked in Grand Central Station. It anyone had bumped into her—highly likely in such a bustling place—the holo-illusion would have shattered. Now, people could bump into Cris as much as they wanted; as long as no one touched his face, the illusion would remain.

She smoothed the bottom of the holo-fabric under the suit jacket, making sure that the image blended seamlessly with the reality of his shirt and suit. She greatly admired the extent of Cris's technical and artistic expertise.

Cris went into the bathroom, looked into the mirror, and began to adjust the mask more carefully over his eyes and nose. Jill watched curiously through the open doorway. He tweaked the holographic image minutely until the transition points between his eyes and Beaumont's became unnoticeable. He did the same for the nostrils.

"Perfect," Beaumont's voice said. The computer-generated lip movement exactly matched the words. "What do you think now, Jill?"

"How are you doing that?" she demanded, studying his mouth.

He laughed Beaumont's laugh. "It's not easy. I sub-vocalize . . . almost like I'm a ventriloquist of sorts, wouldn't you say?"

"It's amazing. You *are* Beaumont." She surveyed him critically from every angle. "I think your head is a little too big, though . . ."

"I know. But I don't think anyone will notice. Remember, they won't be looking for differences."

"You'll never get away with this charade," said the real A.J. Beaumont, now awake. He glared at them as he struggled futilely against his bonds.

"I think it's time for me to get going," said Cris with Beaumont's voice.

"Don't you dare!" the real Beaumont howled.

Jill shivered. She glanced back and forth between the two men, unable to see any difference except their clothing. They could be identical twins. Cris's transformation was uncanny.

"Let's talk in the other room," Jill said. "Having him there listening to our plans makes me uneasy."

"He can't do anything tied up."

"I know, but . . ."

"Okay," Cris said. He led her into his workroom and closed the door.

They could hear Beaumont struggling again to free himself, but Jill wasn't worried. She'd checked the knots and knew they'd hold.

"I don't like waiting here while you go for Marica," said Jill. "You might need backup."

"Someone needs to watch Beaumont."

"I just hope this works." Jill hugged herself, suddenly cold and empty inside. She thought of her parents and of what they'd say when they learned she'd lost her job with Beaumont Industries. Even if Cris did save Marica, that wouldn't change the facts. She'd kidnapped her boss, kept him tied up for two days, and helped a friend impersonate him. When they finally let Beaumont go—and they'd have to eventually—his wrath would know no bounds. She'd be lucky if he didn't press charges against her. She'd be lucky if she ever worked a decent job again.

She found herself wishing that she'd never even heard of Beaumont Industries.

"It'll work," said Cris. His now-blue eyes locked with Jill's. "It's got to. You'll be all right here. Wish me luck."

She nodded, wordlessly praying that nothing would go wrong.

"If anything ever happened to Marica . . ." His Beaumont-holo face looked sad and lost as it mimicked the expressions on the face beneath. "I don't know what I'd do."

Jill put her hands on his shoulders and said reassuringly, "It's going to work." She wished she could feel as positive as she sounded.

She wrapped her arms around him tightly, not wanting to let him go. But she had no choice.

*　　*　　*

A light rain misted along the street in front of the apartment building. Night had just fallen, and the street was almost deserted. A couple with submachine-guns strung across their shoulders were walking a collie along the edge of Fort Tryon Park. A man with a holstered pistol by his right hand and an umbrella in the left hurried toward one of the neighboring apartment buildings.

Cris stared at them sadly. Apparently word of the gang attack the other night had spread. He glanced at the corner where the Beaumont heejee sat. Its auto-defense warning lights sent purple beams rippling across the pavement.

Cristopher opened his umbrella and headed for it. Ten feet away, he used the remote control to turn off the computer's defenses. He felt uneasy as he belted himself into the pilot's seat. He wished he hadn't had to leave Jill behind to guard Beaumont. He wished he'd double-checked the ropes before he left.

He ran through the diagnostic start-up sequence, and everything checked. He powered up the engines and lifted, logging his destination into City Control. It would land him in the nearest empty parking spot. He had about five minutes before he arrived.

Then his face began to itch beneath the holo-mask. Raising a corner, he slipped fingers beneath it to scratch. Once he landed, he told himself, he wouldn't be able to touch his face anymore, so he'd better get it out of his system now.

After a few seconds, the itch came back worse than ever. The first-aid kit under the seat contained antiseptic cream, he knew, but he didn't want to risk messing up his handiwork. A smear of cream over a fiber-optic cable might blur half his face. He decided to try to ignore the itch; maybe it would go away.

The clock read seven thirty. He tried not to wonder where Marica was, or think about how she might already be dead. Instead, he opened the envelope he'd prepared and checked again to make sure the Pacifica disks were safe.

Then he pulled out the ransom note and reread the instructions: "*. . . Bring the Pacifica data on AN-standard one-inch CDRs and stand in front of the old Traveler's Aid Kiosk in Grand Central Station. We will be watching you, so come alone, without any bodyguards. Someone will give you a key to a locker in exchange for the information. If you bring the police, provide false information, or fail to arrive, we will trigger an explosive device attached to Mrs. Beaumont with a remote transmitter.*"

Cris shuddered, thinking of Marica trapped in a locker, surrounded by explosives. If the GANs suspected his masquerade they could easily kill her. He had to be very, very careful. His guts felt twisted in knots, and his mind felt stretched to the breaking point.

A chime sounded. The heejee had reached its destination and began its automatic landing sequence.

Cris monitored as City Control steered him to a rooftop landing pad on a building adjacent to Grand Central Station. As the heejee settled onto a lift, the parking lot's computer requested his credit code. He typed it almost unconsciously.

Once the information had been accepted and the parking fee charged, the lift descended on a mechanism that reminded Cris of a squashed ferris wheel. He exited at ground level, leaving the heejee in its moveable parking space.

Then, taking a hand mirror from his pocket, he checked his face. Alexander James Beaumont looked back, a thirty-year-old cherub with icy blue eyes and thick blond hair. The holo's illusion was perfect. Next Cris checked the power packs attached to his computer-vest: about sixty minutes left. He could do it, he thought, believing it deep inside for the first time. He *would* get away with impersonating A.J. Beaumont.

Picturing Beaumont in his mind, the way he'd looked in person and in all the news reports he'd ever seen, Cris tried to stand the way A.J. would stand, puffing out his chest a little more, tilting his head upward, keeping his arms relaxed and at his sides. *Think like Beaumont,* he told himself.

He put away the mirror and felt inside his pockets, making sure the gun and the envelope with the Pacifica disks were still secure. He took a deep, calming breath. *Think Beaumont.*

It was almost eight o'clock.

He ambled across the street, avoiding the vagrants camped out along the sidewalk, and entered Grand Central's terminal through a side door. He tried to smile a bit, as Beaumont would have, and tried to exude Beaumont's natural charm and confidence, while at the same time having just a trace of worry.

The station's main concourse looked fairly normal. The worst of the commuter rush had ended and all the vendors had closed up shop for the night. Streams of people flowed around him, some headed for the tube-trains, some for the subways, some for the exits. The high, vaulted ceiling arched over one hundred feet overhead, and huge signs on one wall blinked as computers constantly updated arrival and departure times. He could just make out a few zodiac constellations on the peeling paint of the once prized ceiling.

It had been too long since he'd been here, and the once grand architecture struck him now as ever before: the lofty pillars, the wide expanses, the polished marble underfoot. The building reminded him of an era when labor and energy had been cheap enough for beauty to be built into a utilitarian design.

Slowly and deliberately he crossed the concourse to the reach the area that had once been a well-kept waiting room. There were no longer any benches, only a line of cardboard boxes along the back wall that made makeshift hovels for some of the residents of the station.

He felt vulnerable and alone out in the open this way. It occurred to him in a fleeting moment of paranoia that the entire kidnapping could have been an elaborate ploy to lure Beaumont out without his bodyguards. But that didn't make much sense, he realized. If Jade Moon had wanted to kill Beaumont, she'd already had plenty of opportunities.

Why did she act at the wedding, though? he wondered. *With all those people there, she'd been lucky to pull it off.* As Marica's best friend she certainly could have chosen a better time to strike.

His shoulders slumped as he worried. *Think of Beaumont,* he told himself, straightening. *He's always in control, always confident.*

He found the abandoned Traveler's Aid Booth at the entrance to the waiting room. It had been boarded over years ago. He glanced at his watch: one minute after eight. Right on time. People brushed past on their way to the trains, flowing around him as though he were a rock in a river, but nobody seemed to be paying more attention to him than they should be. Turning, he examined neglected kiosk for any notes.

"Hello, honey," said a sultry voice at his elbow.

He whirled—too fast—and found Jade Moon walking toward him. He swallowed nervously, sure she would see through his deception.

"Jade," he said in Beaumont's voice.

"I'm glad to see you." Coming close to him, she smiled as though greeting an old friend, but that mask of green face-paint kept her expression cold and aloof.

When her hand reached out to touch his arm, Cris stepped back, surprised—and afraid of exposure.

"What's wrong?" she asked. The words made as little sense as her tone of friendly concern.

Cris didn't reply. He tried to read the expression in her eyes and failed.

"What's wrong?" she repeated.

"Nothing," he finally answered. "I've got what you wanted right here." He took out the envelope and gave it to her. "How's Marica?"

Jade looked slightly puzzled, but smiled. "Don't worry, Alex, everything's still going according to plan, despite that idiot Morrisey's interference. We've got the bitch wired up and ready to go in one of the lockers."

"Where?"

She pointed toward a ramp leading down to the lower level. Universal signs above it showed the symbol for luggage and an arrow. "I've got the key and the transmitter here." She touched her belt pouch. "You'd better get out of here now. As soon as the GANs realize this stuff's fake, I'll have to detonate the bomb. I don't want you too close when that happens. Darling, it's all working out just like you said it would."

She's working with Beaumont to kill Marica, he realized in shock. Somehow, he managed to hide his expression of disgust behind A.J.'s haughty smirk. Inwardly his thoughts whirled. Everything began to fit together. But why would Beaumont want to help the Green Age? *Unless . . .*

Cris remembered the prenuptial agreement. Beaumont got control of Marica's ships if she died. *Would he kill her just for her shipping fleet?* he wondered. Somehow, that seemed to be the case.

"There's been a change," he said slowly, hoping he'd understood the situation correctly.

"What do you mean?"

He tried to speak calmly, but fear cut through him like a knife. "We can't kill Marica now. There's a problem."

"My god, Alex, after all this planning? Are you kidding?" Jade stared at him so intently that Cris wondered if she'd penetrated his disguise.

"I'll tell you about it later," he said. "There's no time right now. Give me the key to the locker and then you'd better get out of here yourself."

"Are the police here?" asked Jade in alarm, looking around. "You were supposed to keep them out!"

Cris tried to sound reassuring. "Not yet." He thought frantically, trying to piece together everything Jade and Beaumont were doing. "Ellsberg found a legal problem with the prenuptial agreement. Marica has to stay alive a few days longer." He tried to inflect his words the way Beaumont would, and in Beaumont's most authoritative voice he ordered, "Come on, give me the key and get out."

"But I'm not supposed to give it to you till after we examine the disks—"

He held out his hand demandingly. "Now."

Still she hesitated. He wondered if he should grab her and

take it, but there was no way to know if her accomplices were watching, ready to set off the bomb if anything went wrong.

Finally, looking confused, Jade pulled a small key from her handbag and gave it to Cris. As he took it, she seemed to look at his hand a little too intently. He jerked it away and quickly put it inside his pocket.

"Go on, get out of here," he ordered.

She hurried across the room toward the south side, glancing back at him with a strange expression on her green face. Something about his hands had bothered her, he thought. He'd cleaned and manicured them to match Beaumont's as much as possible. Still, they couldn't be exactly like his, and perhaps Jade had sensed their difference.

Cristopher didn't have time to worry. He ran down to the lower level. The key she'd given him had a number stamped on it—R-131—and he searched frantically for the matching locker.

He found it quickly enough: a large bottom locker large enough to fit a body. *Hurry.* His hands were shaking and the key seemed to twist with a mind of its own when he tried to fumble it into the hole. At last he managed to get it into the lock, twisted it, and swung the door wide.

A large steamer trunk lay inside. He pulled it out.

Hoping against hope, he swung its lid up. Marica lay curled inside like a sleeping cat.

He felt her pulse. Still alive, thank God.

He removed the ropes on her feet but couldn't do anything about the handcuffs on her wrists. Then he spotted a small black box wedged in beside her. Gingerly he pulled it out. This had to be the bomb. Labels clearly indicated 'off' and 'on' by a switch, but he hesitated. What if they'd set it to detonate either way? Since Jade Moon had a transmitter, she still might set it off at any moment if she suspected he wasn't the real Beaumont. If he just left the bomb, innocent bystanders could be hurt when the timer triggered it at eight thirty.

Holding his breath, he flipped the switch to 'off.' Nothing happened.

He lifted Marica like a sack of soy meal, shoved trunk and bomb back into the locker, and headed back up to the concourse. Later, he'd phone the police with an anonymous tip and tell them about the bomb. They could dispose of it properly.

Jade Moon felt thoroughly confused as she reached the back part of Grand Central. *What's A.J. doing?* Changing everything after months of planning didn't make any sense. And he's seemed so cold, so distant. He'd seemed different somehow, though she couldn't quite put her finger on what exactly was wrong with him.

Meadowlark met her near the side door, by a deserted news stand. She handed him the envelope. He opened it, pulled out the first two disks, and inserted them into a portable computer he'd brought.

Jade Moon continued to brood. Alex hadn't given her new instructions, and that wasn't like him. Mentally she replayed her conversation with Beaumont. He'd acted almost concerned about Marica. It didn't seem possible, but could he have had second thoughts about killing her?

Jade's fingers curled into fists. That had been the one thing she'd never liked about this scheme. He would be sleeping with pretty little Marica.

"It's good," said Meadowlark. "He kept his word. Give him the key."

"What?" she wasn't sure she'd heard him right.

"It's verified. These plans are real—everything we need, right down to the bacteria's DNA."

"Let me see that!" She grabbed the computer out of his hands and flipped quickly through the entries. They really did look genuine.

Her head began to throb. Nothing made sense any more. Alex had never intended to give the real plans to the GANs. They would ruin his kelp monopoly in months. So why did he do it?

"I'll get the disks to headquarters," said Meadowlark, taking the computer back. "It's going to take all night, but we'll have them duplicated and delivered to every technology company in the world by business hours tomorrow!"

"Great," Jade said numbly.

"Watch your back, okay? Beaumont's bound to call the police once he frees his wife."

"Right," she said, barely listening. "See you soon."

Meadowlark trotted off. They were supposed to separate after they got the disks. According to plan, she was now to give Alex the key to the locker—or blow it up if the data failed inspection—and then return to headquarters via a circular route to make her report.

Only Alex already had the key. Only she didn't get to blow Marica to little pretentious bits.

Only it makes no sense, she thought again. Then she remembered what Marica had said: *"A.J.'s just using you, like he used me."* What was A.J. trying to do? And why had he given the Green Age the real plans to Pacifica?

She ran back into the main concourse in time to see Alex carry Marica out the glass doors to the street. She followed them surreptitiously, a ghost in the night. Still Marica's words echoed over and over in her mind, *He's using you . . . he's using you . . .* Could that brainless bimbo really have gotten to him?

Alex carried Marica into a nearby garage-building and, without a backward glance, went straight to a Beaumont Industries heejee. Jade Moon ducked behind a concrete support pillar to watch.

Setting Marica down, Alex took a screwdriver from inside the heejee and jimmied the handcuffs on Marica's wrists. He threw them aside, and they clattered to the wall. Then, blond head bobbing up and down, he began to massage Marica's hands and face, trying to awaken her. He bent lower, placing his lips on hers not in the kiss of life, but in a sensual kiss.

At last Marica sat up, blinking, crying. Softly, tenderly, he cradled her to him, rocking her, murmuring something.

Jade Moon strained to hear. She felt sick when she realized he was telling her how much he *loved* her.

She bit her lip. Tears filled her eyes. She felt infinitely betrayed, and a lump filled her throat. She swallowed at it, but it wouldn't go away.

Damn them both. She couldn't believe this was happening to her. *I should have killed her after the GANS put her in the trunk, they wouldn't have seen me.*

A.J. picked Marica up again, placed her inside the heejee, and climbed into the pilot's seat. He started powering the engines. As he did, the garage's lift suddenly growled into motion, swinging the heejee around and up, toward the roof.

Jade watched dumfounded. She was certain A.J. had told her he couldn't fly heejees. That's why he always used a chauffeur, even when he went out on the town for the night. *Another senseless lie,* she thought. He'd betrayed her completely and she didn't even know why.

As A.J.'s heejee disappeared from view, the cogs of the machinery bearing it out of the building, she dashed back to the street. A dozen helicabs waited in line by Grand Central's doors. She dove into one and barked instructions to the driver. He powered up and lifted.

"That's it," she said, pointing at A.J.'s heejee as it soared north, "Don't lose them." She had to follow A.J. She had to know what was going on, no matter what.

"Cash or credit?" the cab's driver grunted as he logged their course with City Control.

"Credit." Reaching into her purse for her credit card, she touched the barrel of her gun. It felt as cold, smooth, and familiar as an old lover.

NINETEEN

GOD DAMN you to hell, Morrisey, A.J. thought to himself. *When I get out of this, I'm going to bury you.*

The bumbling artist had royally screwed up months of careful planning. Still, once the stupid ape called in the police, A.J. knew he'd regain control of the situation. He'd twist things around, use Jade Moon to plant some evidence. Before Morrisey knew what hit him, he'd be under arrest for kidnapping Marica himself.

Jealousy made Morrisey abduct her after the wedding. He'd gotten his Green Age friends to help. The tale made sense, and A.J.'s lawyer, Ellsberg, would make a nice witness. If it came to A.J.'s word against Morrisey's, money and connections would make A.J.'s version stick.

A.J. watched Jill warily through half-closed eyes. He slouched in the big armchair, trying to look half asleep. Unfortunately for her, she'd been a witness. He wasn't quite sure yet what angle he'd use against her. *I can start with the videotape of her accepting a bribe from Jade Moon,* he thought with a grim little half-smile.

"Let's see if you made the news," Jill said to him, turning on the television.

One wall darkened, then lit up with a videotext display. As she scanned the reports, A.J. began to wiggle quietly in his bonds again. He'd been quietly flexing his muscles, trying to loosen them, for hours now. He'd managed to loosen the ropes a bit, but he still couldn't pull his hands free from behind his back. Perhaps, if he could just move a bit more to the left . . .

Squirming, he began to lean to one side. When he pushed his hands against the seat for more leverage, his fingertips brushed something hard wedged behind the cushion. Excitement growing, he worked his hands down until his fingers curled around whatever it was. When he tugged it free, he recognized it by feel: A pen.

He didn't think it would do him any good, but the discovery made him reach deeper into the space behind the cushion.

Jill began flipping through TV channels.

His fingers found a coin, then a pencil, and then something longer and just as hard as the pen. It felt slightly sticky along one side. Crumbs of some sort flaked off. Then, beneath his thumb, he felt a razor sharp metal edge at one end that sliced his flesh. With a start he realized what it was—a painter's dirty x-acto knife.

Slowly, carefully, keeping an eye on Jill Washington's back, A.J. Beaumont began to cut himself free.

*　　*　　*

"Cristopher, is that really you?" Marica heard herself ask as if from a great distance. She felt dopey and half asleep, and the man with Beaumont's face and Cristopher's voice made her even less sure of reality.

"Yes, see, it's a hologram," he said, turning A.J.'s face on and off. "I used it to rescue you from Jade Moon. You're safe now. Just lean back and relax, and try not to think about it anymore."

Marica rubbed her eyes and tried to fight the lingering effects of the anesthetic. Hand trembling, she reached out to touch the strange mask Cris wore. He pulled if off and handed it to her.

She wouldn't have recognized Cris, she thought, if he hadn't switched off Beaumont's voice when he carried her out of the train station. It all seemed so blurry and dreamlike. The only thing she remembered clearly was him telling her she was safe.

She turned the mask over and over. A few wires still connected it to Cris's vest. Suddenly the mask came alive in her hands, turning into A.J.'s grinning face, and with a gasp she dropped it. The image blurred with static as it came to rest on her lap. Then it fizzled and went out.

"I had to become Beaumont to get you out of there," he explained. "The GANs who kidnapped you wanted him to deliver the ransom himself."

Cris glanced down at the heejee's computer monitor and suddenly began to scan through the readings intently.

Then he picked the mask up again and slipped it on. Beaumont's face reappeared.

"Please take off the hologram," Marica said. After what Jade Moon had told her about Beaumont, she never wanted to see him again—and certainly didn't want to see Cris made up to look like him.

"Not yet," said Cris very quietly. "I think there's another heejee following us." Looking in his hand mirror, he readjusted the holo-image.

Marica turned in her seat. Heejee traffic filled the sky over New York, moving in stately lines like strings of stars strung along an invisible necklace. She couldn't tell one heejee from another, let alone whether they were being followed. If Cris thought so, she'd take his word for it.

She opened a side vent and took a deep breath. The cool outside air tasted wonderful. A few hours ago, she'd been certain she would die—and now, miraculously, she was alive. It felt very, very good.

"Cris," she said softly. "I . . . I want you to know how sorry I am about the way I treated you. I had time to think, while they held me . . . and I know I've been a selfish, spoiled brat . . ."

Beaumont's face smiled at her with a kindness that could never have belonged to A.J.

"We had a good thing together," she went on, "and I messed it up. It wasn't anything you did, Cris, it was me. I guess I didn't think I deserved anyone as wonderful as you." Squeezing his hand, she felt his sculptor's calluses and knew that it was truly Cris under there. "I *can* change. Will you give me another chance?"

"Marica, you know I will. Don't you know how much I love you?"

She nestled against his shoulder, hugging him. "I love you too, I really do. I just didn't realize how much till it was almost too late." She peered out at the night sky. "It's not over yet, though, is it? There's still Beaumont."

"Don't worry, we're almost to my apartment. When we get there we'll call the police. They'll straighten everything out. We've got A.J. tied up—Jill Washington is watching him."

"God, Cris, I didn't tell you!" Marica sat up. "A.J. planned this whole kidnapping! Jade Moon told me. She joined the Green Age, and then the GANs, on A.J.'s orders. They're lovers. He wanted my shipping companies, so he had Jade suggest to the GANs that they kidnap me. She was going to detonate the bomb no matter what, so the GANs would be blamed for my death and A.J. would get everything!"

"It all makes sense now," Cris said. "Beaumont's a real bastard!"

"But how did you save me?"

"When Jill and I found out Beaumont wasn't going to pay the ransom, I replaced him. Then Jade Moon let slip that she was working with A.J., and I managed to convince her that his plans had changed and you had to be kept alive. If that's her following us, she may have begun to suspect something."

The heejee circled down and landed in front of Cris's apartment. Its spotlights flicked on, flooding the area with light. The streets were empty. As they climbed out, they could see a second heejee descending behind them.

"Go on into the apartment," said Cris, "I'll stay here and see what's going on. If it's Jade, maybe I can convince her to leave."

"She's dangerous. I ought to stay with you."

"Go on," Cris pushed her lightly away from him. "Just hit the bell and Jill will let you in. Hurry."

Marica hesitated a second, then ran across the street, heading for the door. Perhaps Jill could help. She might have a gun, or maybe they could phone the police, or something.

The second heejee landed behind the first.

As Marica rang the bell, the door slid open. A.J. Beaumont stepped out, saw her, and froze in surprise.

"Marica!" he exclaimed. His normally immaculate clothes were disheveled, sweat ran down his face, and his right hand clutched a bloody x-acto knife.

She turned to run, but A.J. grabbed her and yanked her around.

"You're safe," he said, pulling her close. "It's all over, darling."

"Leave me alone!" She struggled against his embrace. "I know you're behind the whole thing. You tried to kill me!"

"How did you—?" He spun her around and pressed the blade of the knife against her throat. "It doesn't matter. For the moment I think you'd better come with me."

Twisting one of her arms behind her back, keeping the knife at her throat, he half carried, half dragged her toward the street. Then he stopped in mid stride. Just ahead stood Cristopher, still looking like his double, his back toward them. Beyond Cris, Jade Moon alighted from a helicab.

"What are you doing here?" Cris asked Jade Moon.

"That's what I was going to ask you, Alex. What do you think you're doing with that little slut? Why the hell—"

Then Jade Moon spotted A.J. and Marica standing near the apartment. As she glanced back and forth at the two Beaumonts, Cristopher turned and saw them, too. A look of shock crossed his face.

Suddenly Jade pulled a gun and aimed it at Marica and Beaumont.

"That's Morrisey!" said the real Beaumont, pointing toward Cris with the knife. "He's wearing some kind of holographic disguise! He found out about our plans, kidnapped me, and freed Marica. Shoot him!"

Instantly Cris pointed toward A.J. and said with Beaumont's voice at its most commanding: "He's really Morrisey, Jade. Look at the way he's fawning over her!"

Jade hesitated, staring back and forth between the two men. In the dazzle of the heejee spotlights the two men looked identical. Jade's eyes focused on the artist's x-acto knife that Beaumont held.

Marica knew she had to act before the real Beaumont thought to tell Jade something only he could know. If she made the correct move now, she could make Jade pick the wrong Beaumont. She had to trick Jade, and Jade would be expecting a trick. Knowing full well what she was doing, she broke loose from Beaumont's hold.

A.J. grabbed her, and she beat at his arm frantically.

"Let go of me, you bastard!" she screamed. "I know what you and Jade were up to! I know you're lovers and tried to kill me! Let me *go*!" She pulled halfway out of Beaumont's arms, reaching toward Cris. "Cristopher, help me!" she yelled.

"You little bitch," said Jade, suddenly smiling. "Trying to trick me. Morrisey's the one who rescued you, you wouldn't betray him. You know that A.J. planned the kidnapping, so now you're trying to trick me into killing him!"

Before Beaumont could speak or move, Jade aimed and pulled the trigger. Behind Marica, he gasped as the bullet hit his chest.

Marica felt a wave of relief. She *had* tricked Jade, but in a more complex way than the woman had realized.

Fingers jerking spasmodically, A.J. seized Marica's arm and dragged her down beside him.

Marica felt herself falling and tried to roll to safety the way she'd once seen Cris do when a statue almost fell on top of him. A.J.'s fingers clawed at her skirt, and she hit the pavement all wrong. Something seemed to rip in her left shoulder and burn like a white-hot needle.

"And now you, my dear sweet stupid friend." Jade fired again, and Marica felt a second burst of pain, this time in her left arm. She screamed.

Then another shot rang out from somewhere behind Marica. Jade staggered as a bullet hit her.

Pain searing her shoulder, Marica wrenched herself onto her side to see the apartment.

Jill Washington leaned against its door. She held a semi-automatic pointed toward Jade. A huge bloodstain covered her chest where a jagged knife-wound ran from her collarbone down to her navel.

Jill fired again. Jade Moon fell back, fired wildly into the ground, and crumpled.

Marica rolled over toward Beaumont. His vivid blue eyes stared up unseeingly at the night. "God," she whispered, putting her head against his blood-soaked chest, but she already knew there would be no sound.

Cristopher ran to Jade and kicked the gun away from her hand. As he leaned down to see how badly she was wounded, Jade reached up and touched his face. Her long fingernails sank beneath through the holo of Beaumont's face.

"No," she whispered. "Marica's not that smart. You had to be the real one. My Alex is—" She coughed and blood spurted out of her nose and mouth. As she coughed again, it became a choking, gurgling sound. Then she lay still.

Marica pried A.J.'s fingers loose from where they still clutched the fabric of her dress—her blue silk wedding dress. *How ironic,* she thought sadly. As she struggled to her feet, she watched Cristopher run to help Jill Washington, who was somehow still standing despite her terrible wound.

Marica gazed down sadly at A.J. All his schemes and planning had gone awry in the end. Pacifica could save the world, he had said, but he wouldn't have let it. He would have used and abused it for his own gain, the way he'd wanted to use her.

Strangely enough, she realized, as A.J.'s widow she now owned Beaumont Industries. She could give the world what it needed, and she would. She would give the world Pacifica.

EPILOGUE

CRISTOPHER STUDIED his holo-painting of the kelp farm against the real one that lay off the *Lady Pecunia*'s port bow. He airbrushed a bit more sienna onto the fronds, trying to catch the correct blend of greenish-brown against deep ocean blue. The water off Rolugo's coast sparkled with a clarity that might soon be echoed around the world, as kelp plantations flourished with the help of Beaumont Industries' Pacifica Project. Other companies had also announced their intention to produce sea farms and ocean energy plants, once the GANs had begun distributing copies of the stolen designs to Beaumont Industries' competitors.

Cristopher didn't mind. He and Marica had decided to allow the world free access to the Pacifica project. Although Beaumont Industries would no longer reap an outrageous fortune from the technology, selling kelp and power would still keep the firm running smoothly in the black for years to come, while boosting the world's economy and ecology. Besides, it would take months for any other company to set up comparable kelp farms. For now, they had a monopoly, though they weren't taking advantage of it the way Beaumont would have.

Cris glanced up as a heejee thrummed overhead. He smiled broadly as it set down on the helipad atop the *Lady Pecunia*. For awhile after Beaumont's death that sound had been almost painful to hear, reminding him of all that had gone on and how he'd almost lost Marica. Things had actually worked out better than he'd hoped. The police assumed Jade Moon was a jilted lover who'd kidnapped Marica and killed Beaumont in a jealous rage. Now that things had settled down, Cris had begun to accept his new life with Marica without fear that he might lose it again.

He took a deep breath of salt-spiced air. He could almost imagine he noticed a difference as the algae did its work. Perhaps someday Pacifica's scientists would find a way to fully reverse the Greenhouse Effect.

"She's arrived," said Marica, coming out of the main salon's doors. She looked so beautiful, with the breeze fanning her hair outward like a golden waterfall, that Cris thought of painting her again.

In his mind's eye he pictured a new work. It would not show the fantasy woman of his previous holos, nor the malicious destroyer of his nightmares. Instead, he would capture the troubled woman who hid behind a too-perfect mask of beauty—the eyes mirroring painful memories and regrets, the stubborn chin, the sad crease around lips that ached for love. At last he'd begun to discover that woman. He was falling in love all over again, but this time with someone real, not just an image.

"Hi there," said Jill, as she followed Marica onto the deck.

"Hi yourself." Cris looked up, winked, and then resumed his painting.

"You look great," said Marica.

"I'm fully recovered, thanks to all those doctors you hired."

"I've been saving the best news for you until you got here," said Marica. "Cris and I have decided to appoint you a vice-president of Beaumont Industries, in charge of our Aerospace Systems Division, if you are willing."

"Are you kidding? Sure. But do you think I really have enough management experience for that?"

"Cris thinks you can handle it with a little training, and I'll see to it that the best people are around to give you any help you need."

Jill laughed. "You really don't need to do this, Marica, but I'm not about to turn it down!"

She stared out at the kelp plantation and Rolugo's shoreline, and a thoughtful look crossed her face. "One thing, though, after all we've gone through. Just don't put me in charge of Pacifica!"

Lightning Source UK Ltd.
Milton Keynes UK
UKOW050640041111

181473UK00001B/162/A